Downfall
By
Margot Kinberg

Grey Cells Press

Downfall

Copyright © 2018 by Margot Kinberg

Cover art Copyright © 2018 by Lesley Fletcher
Visit http://www.lesleyfletcher.com/ for more information about her work.

Cover design and layout © 2018 by germancreative.
Visit https://www.fiverr.com/germancreative for more information about her work.

Dedication

Like everything I do, this book is dedicated to my
family, who make my world complete.

Acknowledgements

I am, as always, grateful to Lynn Mancini, whose editing skill, suggestions, and polishing helped this novel become a finished product in a way I never could have done by myself. I value her skills, and more, than that, her friendship.

Thanks also to Lesley Fletcher, whose artwork graces this cover. Her art is elegant and adds a special touch of beauty to my work. Her friendship enriches me. I am also grateful to germancreative (https://www.fiverr.com/germancreative) whose skill at layout and cover work provided the professional finishing touches to this novel.

I am also grateful to the helpful staff at Valley Forge National Park, who took the time to give me very helpful information about the US National Park Service, and police jurisdictions in those parks.

I'd also like to thank the many helpful members of the online crime fiction reading and writing community. You bring my life more richness than you could know, and you teach me every day. Kathy D., thanks for the title!

Table of Contents

Prologue 2

Chapter One 5

Chapter Two..33

Chapter Three..66

Chapter Four 84

Chapter Five...107

Chapter Six..130

Chapter Seven 156

Chapter Eight 181

Chapter Nine 204

Chapter Ten..232

Chapter Eleven...255

Chapter Twelve...279

Chapter Thirteen 300

Chapter Fourteen...331

Chapter Fifteen..354

Prologue

The sky was so blue it hurt his eyes to look at it. Out there on that beam, three stories up – that was where he wanted to be. Curtis Templeton was going to be king of the world. He was proud of himself, too; he'd managed to get out of school without anyone knowing he was gone. Well, almost nobody knew. He'd been wanting to check out this construction site ever since the weather had started to get warmer, and now that it was nearly summer, it was a perfect day for it. Besides, after what had happened that morning, he wanted to get away. Just get away and think. He was lucky, too. Normally, the construction crew would have been on the site, but they couldn't go any further with what they were doing until the wiring had been completed, and the electricians weren't on site that day. He had the place all to himself. He found a weak spot in the fence surrounding the construction site and squeezed through as he threw a nervous glance around. The last thing he needed was to be spotted while climbing the scaffolding. Slowly at first, but then with growing confidence, he got to what was going to be the second floor of the building. He sat down for a moment on the scaffolding right outside one of the windows and looked inside. Nothing much to see yet – just a big expanse of floor and stark walls. They hadn't started any of the inside plastering and painting yet. It didn't matter, though. He hadn't planned to go inside anyway.

After a short rest, Curtis continued his climb. He'd taken just a few steps when he heard the creak of boards somewhere below him. He stopped to see if the noise had come from his own steps. It hadn't. He glanced down but didn't see anyone. Besides, nobody knew he was up there. Must be a squirrel or something. He listened again for a few minutes, but didn't hear anything more. He climbed a few more steps and, still hearing nothing, turned his attention back to that third-floor beam he wanted to reach. Step by step.

After another short rest, Curtis finally made it to the third floor. It hadn't been easy, but he was fifteen – old enough to get all the way to the top if he'd wanted to. He finally reached the beam he'd been dreaming of sitting on – perched just like a bird over the city street below. When he got to the beam, he slowly straightened up and prepared to walk to the end of it. He knew he could do it; all it took was concentration. Foot in front of foot. He focused carefully and started moving. Then he heard it again – that same noise he'd heard earlier. He stopped for a moment but didn't hear anything. Still, he couldn't help feeling like someone was watching him.

All of a sudden, the world spun out of control as Curtis felt a hard push from behind and lost his balance. He scrabbled frantically to grab something – anything – to keep him from falling, but it was too late. As the coroner's report later said, Curtis Templeton died on impact when his body landed on the street three stories below.

Chapter One

Two Years Later

Mark Donnelly led the three visiting academics on what he called the "red carpet tour" of Second Chance of Cobbs Creek. Located in West Philadelphia, it was a residential program for juvenile offenders. He proudly pointed out the recreation areas, the bedrooms, and the classrooms, and then led his guests through the kitchen and then through the kitchen door into the large yard. A blast of hot, humid July air made the four men catch their breaths, and, as soon as they could, they stepped out of the stifling Philadelphia heat and back into the air-conditioned building.

"Well, that's the whole shootin' match," Donnelly said as he walked with his guests towards the building's front door. "Does anyone have any questions?" Donnelly was a tall, athletic-looking forty-eight years old, with straight brown hair and a small, carefully-trimmed moustache.

"Not about the center, no. You've given us a really thorough tour," said Ben Peterson. He was tall and slender, with thick dark-brown hair, gray eyes and tanned skin. Ben was an Assistant Professor of Criminal Justice at Caesar Rodney College, in suburban Wilmington, Delaware. He and his research colleagues, Jered Carr from Delaware River University, and Joel Williams, from Tilton University, were visiting Second Chance to get information on a study they were conducting on the program's success. Carr was forty-five and of medium build, fair, with slightly thinning salt-and-paper hair. A little taller than Carr and in solid physical shape, Williams was in his early fifties, with graying brown hair. The three of them had met while they were in graduate school and had kept in touch since then. Today, they'd spent the morning at Second Chance's headquarters, and were now just finishing a visit to one of its centers. They were hopeful about the study they were putting together. If it went well, it would look good on all of their records.

"I'm impressed with what I've seen," Jered said. "These young people seem to be productive, stable, and self-controlled."

"The kids who come here really do well," Mark responded, "and the data we've been keeping show that they succeed, too. They do well at our Mayfair and Point Breeze center, too, not just at this one."

"We're looking forward to seeing that data," said Ben.

"I think you'll be impressed with the numbers," Mark answered. "Let's take a quick drive back to headquarters, and we'll look them over."

Mark was determined to give his guests a good impression of Second Chance; the company's reputation was at stake. If the research study produced positive results, Second Chance would have a decent shot at getting contracts from other state and local schools and juvenile justice systems. If they went elsewhere, or if their study showed negative results, Second Chance might have difficulty keeping its existing contracts. The four men left the building and got into Mark's late-model Audi. As soon as they'd closed the doors,

Mark turned the air conditioning on and they were soon on their way back to his office.

Once back at Second Chance's headquarters in Valley Forge, Ben, Jered, and Joel went with Mark to the third floor of the building, where the administrators' offices were located. They were soon seated at a small table in Mark's office.

"So," he said once they were settled, "What would you like to know?"

"Well, I'd like to know about recidivism rates," Williams said. "Do you have any data on how many of these kids stay out of the justice system once they leave Second Chance?"

"That's a fair question," Mark answered. "I've asked Lauren to put together a few reports for you to look at. There's information there on graduation rates, incarceration rates, and a lot of other data that I think will help you. Just a second and I'll ask her to join us."

Mark picked up his phone and within five minutes, there was a tap on the office door and Jered's wife, Lauren Carr, came in. She'd been working for

Second Chance for five years. In fact, it was through Lauren that Jered, Ben and Joel were introduced to Donnelly and the Second Chance programs. As she seated herself at the table, Lauren included the whole group in a friendly smile. "Hi, everyone," she said. Joel and Ben each greeted her warmly, and Jered smiled a greeting at her.

For the next twenty minutes, the group went over the details of the reports Lauren had brought with her. What the group was hearing sounded good, too. It seemed that students who attended Second Chance programs were more likely to graduate from high school, less likely to go to prison, and less likely to abuse drugs or alcohol. Maybe there was something to these for-profit alternatives. Ben, Joel and Jered looked at each other and Ben gave a brief nod.

"This looks terrific," Jered said. "I think Second Chance would make a great choice for us to profile in our study. What do you think, Ben?"

"This is really helpful," Ben responded. "I appreciate your being willing to share this with us. What's your view, Joel?"

"I think this looks like a very solid program and could make for a great paper. Thanks for this data."

"Oh, my pleasure," Mark said. "We're glad you're interested in our program. You've got solid reputations as scholars, and, frankly, we can use the good reputation that goes with a formal study."

"Then I think we have a partnership," Jered said with a smile.

"If you don't mind," said Ben, "I'd like to take copies of these reports with me, so the three of us can get started."

"That'd be fine," Mark said. He rose, and the others followed suit. After handshakes all around, Joel, Ben and Jered took their leave. Once they'd gone, Lauren said to Mark, "I think they're pleased with what they saw."

"Good," Mark answered, "We can use the credibility from a good report."

"Don't worry about that. I think our numbers will impress them."

The three visitors took the elevator down to the building's lobby to get a last few minutes of air-conditioned comfort before heading to their cars. As they prepared to leave the building, Jered said, "I know you have to get back to Tilton, Joel, but do you have time for an early dinner?"

"Sorry, no. I've got an eight o'clock class and I want to get back at a reasonable hour."

"Ben?"

"I can't either," said Ben. "I'm going to a Blue Rocks game tonight with a couple of people." Ben liked baseball, and although he was a Phillies fan, he sometimes went to see the minor-league Wilmington Blue Rocks play. Frawley Stadium, their home field, was closer to where he lived than Philadelphia was.

"OK, we'll do it another time. But before we all separate, I do want to know what you guys think of Second Chance," Jered said.

"It looks like an interesting program," Ben answered. "I think it's a good choice for our study."

"It seems like a solid choice," Joel added, "It's got a decent reputation, the findings look good, and the kids seem settled and stable. I'll be interested to see if those numbers hold up when we really look at them."

"So will I," Ben said slowly.

[11]

Jered was quick to notice his friend's tone. "You think there's a problem?"

"No, I didn't say that. I'm just always a little suspicious when things are too neat, if you know what I mean." His companions nodded. None of the three men knew how accurate Ben's judgment would turn out to be.

Three Months Later….

Jered Carr's office phone rang insistently. With a grunt of annoyance, he picked it up and growled, "Hello, this is Jered Carr."

"What's the matter, Jered. Did I interrupt something?" Ben Peterson's voice dragged Jered from the papers he'd been grading.

"Oh, no – sorry, Ben. I'm in the middle of grading some Introduction to Criminology papers, and they're driving me crazy."

"Been there. Done that. Well, I wanted to talk to you about our Second Chance data. If this is a bad time, though…."

"No, not really. In fact, it would actually be a good idea for me to take a break."

"Great! I've found out something that I think you should know. Do you think that you and Joel and I could have a three-way conversation about it?"

"Sure, I was going to ask you about doing that, anyway."

"OK, I'll call Joel and then call you back."

"All right."

The two men finished their conversation, and then Jered hung up the phone and returned, rather reluctantly, to the papers he'd been grading.

Ben hung up the phone slowly. Maybe he was worrying too much. After all, what he'd found could have happened in any program. Still, it was odd. As he reread what he'd found, he couldn't help thinking of his younger brother, Doug. As a teenager, Doug had been arrested for joyriding and had been sent to a juvenile prison. After he'd been released, he'd gone steadily downhill, despite the support that Ben and their parents had tried to provide. Doug had ended up getting arrested twice more before his twenty-first birthday. Right now, he was in prison for breaking and entering, assault, and illegal possession of firearms - charges connected with a robbery he and some of his friends had committed. He would be in prison for three more years before his case was up for a parole hearing. Ben believed that if Doug had had the opportunity to get involved in a solid program when he was younger, he might have made better choices. Ben knew that no program could help everyone. Still, he had wanted to believe that an option like Second Chance could prevent other young people from making the same mistakes that Doug had. That was one of the main reasons he was upset at what he'd found out.

Now, he looked again at his computer screen and ran his hand through his thick dark brown hair. Maybe he just needed some more background. All of a sudden, Ben realized that he'd been sitting staring and thinking when he was supposed to have gotten his colleagues on the phone. He really needed some input on what he'd found. With a shake of his head, he picked up his office phone again.

"Criminal Justice Department, Joel Williams speaking."

"Hi, Joel, it's Ben Peterson. How are you?"

"Doing great! How are you?"

"Fine, thanks. Listen, you got a minute?"

"Sure, what's up?"

"It's about the Second Chance project."

"What's on your mind?"

"I was going over some of the records for the program, and I've found something I'd like to talk about with you and Jered. Do you have time for a three-way call?"

"Sure. I have a meeting coming up, but it's not for half an hour yet."

"Great. Hold on, and I'll get Jered on the phone." Williams agreed, and Ben reconnected with Carr. In a moment or two, the three men were on the line together.

"So, what's on your mind, Ben?" Carr asked.

"Well, I was going over some of the background from Second Chance that Lauren sent me. It turns out that their centers have really strict attendance policies, so they account for every kid."

"That makes sense," Williams said. "So, what's the problem?"

"Well, it's just this," Peterson responded. "I was surfing around on the Internet to see if there might be any stories about Second Chance in the area newspapers. Did you two know that a Second Chance student died about two years ago?"

"No, I didn't know that," Carr said.

"Well, it never made the front page or anything. Apparently, Curtis Templeton – that was the student's name – was hanging around in a construction zone near the Second Chance center we visited. He was climbing around on some scaffolding and fell – died on impact."

"That's awful," Williams said. "But doesn't the center have fairly strict supervision? Wouldn't someone have known he wasn't on campus?"

"Exactly. That's what I don't understand."

"Well, kids do play hooky and they get away with it," Carr said.

"Yeah, I know that, but at some point, with a place that small and secured that well…"

"Someone should have noticed that this boy wasn't there," Williams put in.

"That's what I think," Peterson responded. "Our study is going to have to include their supervision. If somebody can be off campus without anyone knowing about it, I don't know how comfortable I'd be putting our names on the study without making that clear in the writeup."

"I agree," Williams said. "Can you find out some more about this case, and then let us know?"

"Sure," Peterson said. "I'm interested, anyway."

"I can ask Lauren about it, if you want," Carr said. "She might know something."

"Thanks," Peterson said. "And I'll do some background reading – see if there was ever a police report filed, that kind of thing."

"Sounds good," Williams said. "I'll go over the school's handbooks and policy statements and see what kind of supervision they're actually supposed to be providing."

"Sounds as though we've got a plan," Peterson said. "How about if we talk again in a week and see what we've come up with?"

The two other men agreed, and the conversation was soon ended.

Two hours later, Jered Carr had finished the papers he was grading, and was ready to head home. He packed some articles he was reading and some of the paperwork he'd gotten from Second Chance into his briefcase and shut down his computer. With a quick glance around his office, he picked up his briefcase and pulled his tweed jacket from its hook beside his bookshelves. He left his office, locking the door behind him and putting on his jacket as he went. A brisk autumn wind was whistling across campus and creating small tornadoes of fallen leaves as Jered walked to his black Chevy. He pulled his coat a little tighter around him and picked up his pace. When he got to the car, he absently tossed his briefcase into the back seat and settled himself with a grunt into the driver's seat.

As he pulled out of the parking lot and drove towards the campus' main entrance, Jered couldn't help thinking about Curtis Templeton, who'd been only fifteen when he died. His parents must have been devastated. He couldn't even imagine what they must have gone through. Jered didn't have any children of his own; he'd never had a strong desire to be a father, and Lauren hadn't really wanted children, either. Neither had his first wife, Cindy. But he could guess the parents would have been broken up. Well, he'd ask Lauren about it when he got home. For now, he would have to concentrate on traffic. Fortunately, it wasn't a long trip. The Carrs lived in Horsham, about twenty minutes from Jered's office.

Lauren Carr heard her husband pull into the driveway of their small, brick, three-bedroom home. She walked into the living room as she heard the front door bang.

"Hi," she said as Jered walked in.

"Hi, yourself," Jered said. "How was your day?"

"Way too long – yours?"

"Not too bad."

"Jered, do you mind if we just order takeout pasta and salads tonight? Honestly, I've had a hell of a day and I don't feel like cooking. It doesn't like you want to cook, either."

"No – I mean, yeah, takeout's fine."

Lauren looked closely at her husband, then said, "What's on your mind?"

"Sorry – just thinking about something I found out at work today. And actually, I have a question for you."

Lauren raised her eyebrows expectantly.

"You get all the reports from the different Second Chance centers, right?"

"I don't always, but the office does. Why?"

"I'm wondering about a student named Curtis Templeton. He was at the Cobbs Creek center."

"You mean that kid who fell off the scaffolding at the construction site? What a terrible accident."

"I know. Ben and Joel and I just found out about it today, and since we're doing this study, we want to know as much as possible about what goes on at Second Chance. When Ben checked the attendance records, it turned out that Curtis Templeton was recorded as being in his classes that day. It's just weird that the school didn't seem to know he wasn't there."

"Well, I know there are lots of security procedures at the centers, but maybe he found a way around them. Kids do sneak out of school."

"Yeah, maybe you're right. Maybe that's how it happened." Jered shrugged and sat down heavily on the sofa. It had been a long day for him, too. Then he realized he hadn't even asked Lauren about her day. "I'm sorry. I've going on and on. What happened to you today?"

"It was nuts all day long...."

While Jered and Lauren Carr were enjoying their takeout, Joel Williams was staring at his home computer screen, scrolling through Second Chance's policy statements as he absently took a bite of the half-eaten turkey sub that lay on its opened paper wrapper on the desk next to the computer. With his wife at a meeting of the local Professional Women's Association, Williams didn't have a dinner partner, so he'd stopped at the Yellow Submarine for a sandwich.

Soon, he found what he was looking for: the policy about leaving the residence grounds. According to Second Chance's documentation, policy required that students not leave the grounds without at least one staff member or one designated parent or guardian. If Ben was right, then somehow, this Curtis Templeton had found a way to be marked as present in his classes while he was really at a construction site, two blocks from the school. What was odd about it was that according to school policy, attendance was taken five times a day: first thing in the morning; during every class; at each meal; once in the evening; and at one other random time each day. There were only twenty-five students at that center, too, so it shouldn't have been difficult to keep track of one of them, unless Curtis Templeton had been a lot smarter and sharper than anyone guessed. Williams made some notes for himself and resolved to give Ben a call the next morning. The two of them and Jered were going to have to decide what to do about their Second Chance research. If their study was going to be accurate, they might have to call attention to what seemed like a serious lapse on the part of the center's staff. On the other hand, Williams knew how adept teenagers can be at sneaking around and avoiding getting caught. If this kid was especially sharp, Williams could see how he might have slipped out without being seen. Of course, a construction site was irresistibly attractive to young people, too, so it made sense that Curtis would have been there. Beyond that, Williams couldn't go at the moment.

After a solid hour and a half of reading through online articles, Ben Peterson found that he'd learned precious little about the death of Curtis Templeton. The online archives of the local newspapers hadn't contained more than brief paragraphs, and although there'd been a few letters to the editor calling for better supervision of young people and more military-style reform schools, there hadn't been much public notice given to Curtis' death. Maybe Jered could find out more, since he lived closer to the center. He might be able to visit the school again, maybe talk to some people. Ben would send him an email about that. For now, he bookmarked a few of the Internet sites he'd found, and made a few notes. Then, glancing at the time displayed on his computer, Ben realized that it was past eleven and he had a nine o'clock class the next morning. He yawned, stretched, and turned off the computer.

At six-thirty the next morning, Jered Carr shuffled sleepily towards the kitchen for his morning tea. As he fumbled with the kettle and the water, he heard the soft buzz of televised voices. He poked his head into the living room where his wife was curled up on the couch watching the early morning news.

"Morning," he said.

Lauren looked up and smiled.

"I'm making some tea. You want anything?"

"No, thanks, I've got to get into the office. I'll grab some coffee or something on the way."

"All right."

"Are you going to the office today?"

"Yeah, for a bit. Then I'm going over to Cobbs Creek."

"Still worried about that kid who died?"

"Well, yeah, a little. I just want to ask a couple of questions about it. Plus, I want get some more information for our paper."

"Well, let me know if you need anything from headquarters, OK?"

"Thanks, I will."

Lauren nodded, then hurried upstairs to get showered and changed for work while Jered was called back to the kitchen by the whistling tea kettle. In a few minutes, he'd settled himself at the computer to check his Email. Along with the usual emails (upcoming departmental meetings, questions from students, and other normal work-related issues), he saw one from Ben Peterson:

Hey, Jered,

I wasn't able to find out much about Curtis Templeton's death. Since you're a little closer to the center, do you think you'd have time to ask around? Maybe visit the center? I'd sure appreciate it
- Ben

Jered thought for a moment. It was weird that Ben hadn't found anything in the online papers, but maybe one boy's death just didn't make that much difference in a city. Well, it wouldn't be a big problem to at least ask a couple of questions. He dashed off a quick reply to Ben, agreeing to see what he could find out, since he was going to the center anyway. Then, he turned his attention to the rest of his messages.

Joel Williams hung up his office phone with a muttered epithet. This was the third time he'd been put on hold, only to be told that he wasn't talking to the right person. He'd arrived at his office a few minutes early this morning, thinking he might talk to someone at Second Chance about their policies and procedures. Even if he hadn't wanted to learn more about Curtis Templeton's death, he would at least want to talk to someone about how those policies were established and enforced. It was an important part of the research team's study of Second Chance, but it seemed that nobody there could tell him anything about the process. He'd first called the center they'd visited, but had been told he had to call headquarters. His call had been transferred to two different offices there, and neither person he spoke to was authorized to tell him anything. The only information he could find was what was already online. It looked as though he was going to have to ask Jered to look into this question, too. In the meantime, Williams would look through some online journal articles he'd found that mentioned Second Chance. He doubted they would say anything about Curtis Templeton, but they might give a clue about the school's policies.

Five minutes later, Williams slapped an exasperated hand on his desk. He'd forgotten another important source of information – the School District of Philadelphia's Office of Charter Schools. Second Chance offered high school diplomas through its centers, so those centers would have to be approved by the School District of Philadelphia. "Some researcher," Williams grumbled as he went to the District's website. Once there, he found the listing for Second Chance, and began to read the school's most recent accreditation reports. The accreditation team had last visited the school two years ago – two months before Curtis Templeton's death. That report would have the most updated information, so Williams decided to download and print it.

He also found out that the Second Chance centers were funded by the City of Philadelphia as an alternative to juvenile prison. He made a note to himself to have the team follow up with whoever it was in the city government who was responsible for that contract. That office might have the company's paperwork, and that would be good background information to have.

Jered Carr's office key fumbled in the lock as he struggled to open his office door before his phone stopped ringing. He rushed across to the phone, picked it up and barked, "Hello!"

"Hi, Jered, it's Joel Williams. It sounds like I caught you at a bad time."

"Sorry about that. I was having trouble with the lock on my office door and had to run to pick up the phone."

"Do you want me to call you back?"

"No, that's fine. What's up?"

"Well, I was looking over a few things about Second Chance's policies and some other things, and I found out some interesting information. I'm hoping you'll be able to follow up at the center or at headquarters, since you're closer than I am."

"OK, shoot."

"OK," Williams glanced quickly at some notes he'd made for himself. "It looks as though Second Chance was last re-accredited about two months before Curtis Templeton died. In order to get that re-accreditation, the center had to show how it accounts for its students. If Curtis Templeton left the school on the day he died, he would have to either have been accompanied, or snuck out and been pretty slick about it."

Carr thought for a moment. "So, are you saying someone from the Cobbs Creek Center might have been with him?"

"Well, that's the thing. He'd have needed to have someone with him to leave the building unless he was a lot savvier than he probably was."

"What are the procedures for leaving the building?"

"That's what I was going to ask you about. The accreditation report doesn't give a lot of detail about what, exactly, is supposed to happen. I was hoping maybe you could make some time to stop in at the Cobbs Creek Center and talk to them. I tried calling, but I got the runaround."

"Sure. Ben already asked me about doing the same thing, and I was going there anyway. There's not much about Curtis Templeton's death in the online newspaper archives, either."

"I'm glad you're going over there. I'd love to find

out what Second Chance's procedures actually are and how well this center complies with them. I think that might be important."

"Joel, do you think there might be something wrong about this kid's death?"

"Hard to say. I mean, teenagers are experts at sneaking around when they want to. It wouldn't be the craziest thing in the world that this one managed it. But it seems to me a school like this ought to have kept better track of him."

"Yeah, seems that way to me, too, but you're the former cop. I'm just an ex-parole officer – not the same thing."

"Well, I think you have good instincts, Jered. Let me know what you find out, OK?"

"Yeah, I'll call you as soon as I learn anything."

"Good, and I'll be up there in a day or two, anyway. I want to talk to some of the students who've finished the program, see how they're doing. A bunch of them still live in Philadelphia, so I'm going to do some interviews."

"That's a fantastic idea."

"Thanks. I got a few names and called them to see if we could meet."

"Sounds great."

"I hope it will be."

Williams glanced at his watch, then quickly said, "Sorry, Jered, but I'm going to have to go. I'm ten minutes late for a School of Social Sciences meeting."

"No problem. Talk to you soon."

"Right. 'Bye."

Williams hung up the phone and, as quickly as he could, grabbed his windbreaker from the hook on his office door, tearing its hang loop in the process. Muttering angrily, he shoved his arms in the jacket's sleeves, grabbed his briefcase and hurried out, slamming the door in his haste. He barreled down the hall, nearly colliding with Noelle Sanders, the department secretary.

"You OK?" she asked.

"Sorry, Noelle," Williams called over his shoulder. "I'm late for the -"

"- School of Social Sciences meeting, right? Well, don't kill yourself on the way."

"Thanks, I'll be careful."

Noelle shook her head as she watched Williams'
retreating figure, then turned back to the LCD
projector she'd been transporting to one of the
classrooms.

Chapter Two

Williams was lucky. The School of Social Sciences meeting hadn't really begun yet when he got there. These things never started on time, so he was able to slide into a seat at the back of the room before anyone noticed him. He whispered hellos to the people next to him, and settled in. After a minute or two, Dean Alicia Cardenas approached the podium and greeted the group.

"Thanks, everyone, for being here. I know we're all busy. I wanted to share some exciting news with you. Our school is about to receive a three-million-dollar donation!" There were murmurs of, "That's amazing" and "Wow!" Several of the faculty members started to talk among themselves, and the noise level rose. Then, after a minute or two, everyone quieted down, so that the dean could continue.

"Let me give you some background, and then we'll talk about what this will mean for us. YouthPromises would like to set up a center for research into juvenile offenders, and they've selected our School of Social Sciences as the right place to house that center!"

There was scattered applause for a moment. Then the dean went on. "For those of you who didn't know, YouthPromises has been at the forefront of alternatives to juvenile prison. They have several halfway houses and other facilities, and they've been working on developing some adventure camps and other short-term programs. They want some data on how young people do in alternative programs as opposed to the traditional juvenile justice system, and that's where we come in. Our school can take a look at what's out there from four or five different perspectives, with several of our departments involved."

Williams liked what he was hearing so far. His own background reading had led him to suspect that effective alternative programs could be viable options for young people. The traditional juvenile justice system wasn't the answer for every case. That was part of the reason he'd wanted to do the study of Second Chance. He brought his mind back to what the dean was saying.

"…a partnership between our school and YouthPromises will be good for everyone. And we'll be bringing in people from other institutions to make sure we have the expertise we need. Now, does anyone have any questions?"

A dozen hands went up. The first to be called on was Marguerite Southman, from Psychology.

"What will the faculty's role be in this new center?" She always got directly to the point.

"A lot of this is still being worked out," the dean hedged. "But rest assured, our school and the center will be connected. As we move on, we'll keep everyone informed about opportunities for you to be involved."

Jerry Quillian from Sociology was next. "You mentioned bringing experts in. Don't we have people here who can do the research? Isn't that the point?"

"Absolutely," the dean reassured him. And some of you will be a part of this. But we'll also be depending on input from other experts, too."

"Can you clarify that?" Quillian persisted.

"Of course. I mean that we'll have people from YouthPromises, people from a few other alternative programs, and some other interested parties."

The next question came from Shirley Mizzello, one of Williams' colleagues in Criminal Justice. "You talked about links and connections between the school and the center. How will that impact our students?"

"That's a great question," Cardenas said. "The center will offer us the chance to improve and update the learning experiences students have. We'll be filling you in more on how that will work in the coming weeks and months. But yes, this will have an important role to play in what our students experience."

With that, the dean ended the meeting. There was a buzz of conversation as people left the room in twos and threes. Williams had just about reached the door when he heard a voice behind him. "Are you on your way back to your office, Joel?" It was Shirley Mizzello.

"Yeah, I am."

"Do you have a few minutes to talk?"

"Sure." Shirley thanked him, and they fell into step together. Neither said much as they made their way back to Carlton Hall, where the department was located.

When they got there, Williams said, "My office? Yours?"

"Yours is closer."

Williams nodded and the two went into his office and sat down.

"What's on your mind?" Mizzello was usually upfront about what she was thinking, but not this time.

"It's the new center. I've got some concerns about it, and I wanted to sound you out."

"Shoot."

"For one thing, did you notice that Alicia dodged the question about faculty involvement?" Williams nodded. He had noticed that, and he wasn't surprised that Mizzello had, too. She'd been an attorney and then a judge before coming to academia, and she was sensitive to those nuances.

"And then there was my question about the impact on students. I'm wondering if this will mean our curriculum has to change."

Williams thought for a moment. "That hadn't occurred to me during the meeting, Shirley. Are you saying you think we'll have to redo the programs?"

"I don't know about that. But it always concerns me when I think there might be a question of academic freedom."

"You see this new center as interfering with academic freedom?"

"I'll admit it, Joel," Mizzello's green eyes met Williams'. "It makes me uneasy to think the center could have an influence on what we teach. There've been a lot of academic freedom cases in the last few years, and they're often a mess – really complicated. I hope this doesn't turn into one."

"You really think that'll happen?"

"I'm just saying it could, that's all. Did you get the same idea?"

Williams thought for a moment. "I'm not sure, now that you mention it. Alicia's generally a supporter of faculty. But she's also an administrator. If the word comes from On High that we need to change our curriculum, well, who knows? But, let me ask you this. Don't we redo our curriculum periodically anyway?"

Mizzello shook her head a little. "That's the thing. We do need to look over our courses and programs from time to time and make adjustments. But we're the ones – the faculty – who do that. I don't want someone else determining what we include. Otherwise it could violate faculty policy."

"I agree with you in principle," Williams said. "Hopefully it won't come to that."

"I hope so, too. But I think we need to consider what we'll do if it does."

"Do you have a plan in mind?"

"No, not yet. But we may need one. I'm going to think about this and get back to you, if that's all right."

"Yes, of course."

"Thanks. I might need your help." As Mizzello got up to leave, Williams began to wonder what he was signing up to do. She was usually easygoing, which made her pleasant as a colleague. But she also had a sharp legal mind. She wouldn't easily tolerate anything she saw as a policy violation.

Williams turned his computer on and looked down at his desk. There were the notes he'd made on Second Chance. He looked them over again and added to them as he thought about what the dean had said. If companies like YouthPromises and Second Chance showed strong success rates, they were going to be a force to be reckoned with in education. He hadn't thought about the impact on higher education, but there was bound to be one. That angle would need to go in this study he and Ben and Jared were doing. Williams put his hand on his office telephone for a moment, then he thought better of it. Jered was in the middle of things, and he guessed Ben was, too. It would wait until their next meeting.

Ben Peterson dismissed his students from class and slowly walked back to his office. This group of students was one of the more difficult classes he'd had in the last few years. A lot of them tried hard, but they just didn't seem to be getting a good grasp of the material and it was already October; the semester was a month old. Of course, it was hard to sex up technology in criminal justice. Most of his students imagined that being a detective was a matter of interviewing witnesses and chasing "bad guys," at least at first. They didn't realize how much of criminal justice relies on a slow process of information gathering and organization, and for that, you need computers. Fortunately, he was going to a seminar next month on some teaching strategies. He was hoping to pick up some new ideas.

For now, he had other plans. Ben had decided to check out Second Chance's reputation with the local police. It wasn't going to be easy, because individual juvenile records were sealed, but maybe he could find out whether there was a pattern of police being called in frequently, or other signs that the students at Second Chance weren't being supervised as they should be. So, when he returned to his office, Ben immediately began an Internet search of local newspapers' police blotters. After an hour of searching, he hadn't come up with very much. From what he found in the newspaper archives, Second Chance of Cobbs Creek certainly didn't seem to be a hotbed of criminal activity. He couldn't find much at the Mayfair or Point Breeze centers, either. Whatever the truth was about Curtis Templeton's death, there didn't seem to be any signs that Second Chance had serious systemic problems.

Jered Carr pulled into the parking lot of Second Chance of Cobbs Creek. He wasn't sure what kind of a reception he'd get. After all, people generally aren't happy about discussing in detail how a school failed so miserably at keeping a child safe. Still, he was hoping to be able to get at least some answers. Apart from the metal detector at the front door, the building that housed Second Chance of Cobbs Creek looked like many of the other rowhouses in the Cobbs Creek area. The school actually occupied three rowhouses that had been knocked together to create larger spaces so despite its outward appearance, the inside of the school gave the sense of space and air.

Carr closed the door behind him and nodded a greeting to the security guard seated in the foyer.

"Can I help you?" the guard asked.

"Yes, thanks," Carr said, not quite sure where to begin. "Could I speak to your center director?"

"Just go to the office and ask them, and they'll let our director know you're here."

Carr thanked the guard and crossed the foyer to an opened door labeled "Main Office."

"Can I help you?" asked the student aide who served as the receptionist.

Carr said, "Is your center director available?"

"Mr. Dawson, he ain't – isn't – here right now. You want to talk to Mr. Adler? He's the assistant director."

"Sure, that'd be great."

The young girl nodded, said, "You can wait here while I get him," and soon disappeared into the hall. Carr took a seat on one of the uncomfortable-looking small chairs and glanced around him as he waited. The office looked like so many other small school offices he'd visited. There were motivational posters on the wall, a small computer and telephone at the reception desk and what looked like mailboxes for the staff along one of the walls.

In a minute or two, Carr heard footsteps coming down the hall, and a moment later, the teenage receptionist came in, followed by a man Carr took to be the assistant director. Taller than Carr, with limp dark-blond hair and wire-rimmed glasses, the man stuck his hand out.

"I'm Sheldon Adler, assistant director here."

"Nice to meet you. I'm Jered Carr. I'm part of a research team that's doing a study of Second Chance."

Adler thought for a moment. "Oh, yeah, now I remember. If it's the same thing I'm thinking of, didn't somebody from your team visit here a couple of months ago?"

"That's right. Mark Donnelly, from your headquarters, gave us a tour."

"Now I remember. I wasn't there that day, but Tim Dawson, our director, told me about it, and I saw the paperwork on your study, too. What can I do for you?"

"Well, we're still working on our study, and I've got a couple of questions if you have some time."

"Sure, why don't we get some coffee and chat in my office?"

"Sounds good. Thanks."

Carr thanked the receptionist, and then followed his
host down a short hall to a small room on the right
side. With a gesture, Adler indicated the door and
the two men went into the office. Carr took a seat
on one of two utilitarian chairs near the desk while
Adler walked over to a small end table and poured
coffee from a coffeemaker into two Styrofoam cups.
"Do you take milk or sugar?"
"No, thanks – just black."
Adler nodded and passed one of the cups to his
guest. Then, he took a seat at his desk and said, "So,
how can I help you?"
"I'm wondering if I could ask you a few questions
about some of your procedures. I want to get a
really clear picture of how the center works."
"OK. I may not be able to answer everything, but
I'll try."
"Thanks. One of the things that can be a real issue
in alternative schools is safety and security. How do
you monitor the students?"
"Well, we've got a ratio of just five students to each
staff member. We've got twenty-five kids here right

now, and five staff members besides myself and Tim Dawson. Three of them live onsite, and the other two come in during the day to teach."

"And what about when students leave the building?"

"They don't leave the building without one of the staff members, or a parent or guardian."

"How do you check on that?"

"Any student who leaves the building has to sign out, and the responsible adult signs out, too."

Jered knew he might be taking a risk, but he decided to probe just a little more. "Must be hard monitoring a group of savvy teenagers."

"Yeah, it has its days, but we keep track of them pretty well. We do a head count first thing in the morning, at every class and meal, and in the evening, too. We also do a random check every day. Besides, the windows and doors are alarmed, and the kids don't know the code. We change the code regularly, too. So, it'd be pretty hard for one of them to leave without anyone knowing about it."

"Sounds thorough." Jered paused, then went on. "I don't know if you know this, but in another life, I was a parole officer. I've worked with a bunch of young people in my time, and I learned how slick they can be about sneaking out when they want to. That ever happen here?"

"Oh, I know what you mean about being slick, but we're pretty careful here. Besides, these kids know that they've got two options: follow the rules or go to juvie."

"I'll bet that's a powerful motivator."

"It is."

"I guess I asked mostly because when my teammates and I were doing some background reading on Second Chance, we read about what happened to Curtis Templeton."

"Curtis Templeton? Oh, yes, of course. If you know about that, then no wonder you had questions about our security. Well, I'm sorry to have to say it, but not all of our students settle in and learn to make wise choices. Curtis never really did."

"Can you tell me about him?"

"I don't see that it has anything to do with your study, really. Curtis was here because he was one of those defiant kids who can't handle authority. He got into fights, the whole thing.'"

"So, what happened to him?"

"Not one of our prouder moments," Adler said, ruefully shaking his head. "Curtis managed to slip out and must have been drawn to that construction site – you know about that, right? – like a moth to flame. He was probably trying to show off and fell. It was pretty awful, really."

"So I've heard."

"But listen, don't get the wrong impression. That event wasn't typical of the kind of thing that goes on here. I wouldn't want you to get the wrong idea."

"I understand. These tragic things happen."

Adler's face, which had tensed up at the mention of Curtis Templeton, relaxed a bit. "Exactly. It was a terrible, tragic thing, but it was one incident."

"Well, I appreciate your telling me about it. Now, maybe you would give me a little background on the kinds of classes you offer here?"

"Sure. We're a charter school, so we have to meet School District of Philadelphia standards. Here, let me show you some of our classes."

Adler opened one of his desk drawers and drew out a booklet. He flattened it on his desk and for the next few minutes he and Carr discussed the classes that were described in it. Then, Adler glanced at his watch and said, "I don't mean to rush you, but I've got a meeting with a parent."

"Of course. I should be going, anyway."

Carr straightened up to leave the office. As he stood, he slid some reports Adler had given him into his briefcase. "I sure appreciate your time," he said to Adler.

"Oh, my pleasure. Anything I can do…"

"Thanks. We'll be in touch, if that's OK."

"Sure, that'd be fine."

The two men shook hands and Adler walked Carr to the door of his office. Once Carr had left, Adler returned to his desk and sat silently for a few moments, idly tapping the end of a pencil against his desk. This research team could cause him some severe problems. He'd been prepared for their visit, and he'd done a good job, he thought, of answering their questions. Yes, that part had gone well enough. But he was hoping they wouldn't come back with more questions. That could cause real trouble.

[49]

Adler's thoughts were interrupted by the insistent vibration of his cell phone. He pulled it out of his pants pocket and glanced at the screen. Of course! Just his luck! It was his ex-wife Valerie. He angrily pushed the "Reject" button on his phone and put the phone back in his pocket. He had no desire to speak to that bitch after she and her sleazy lawyer had taken him for practically everything he had when they divorced. Money-hungry tramp! He'd be paying court costs and lawyer fees for years because of her, and it wasn't as though he earned top dollar. Making ends meet was enough of a challenge without that added debt. Well, at least he'd figured out a way around that problem. Still, even seeing Valerie's name pop up on his phone screen was enough to give him a headache. He would call her when he was damned good and ready.

Joel Williams glanced at the time on his office computer. There were still fifteen minutes before his next class – enough to get his mail. He decided to stretch his legs and stop at the main departmental office to pick up his mail and his messages.

"Did you get to your meeting OK?" Noelle asked when she saw him.

"A little late, but yes, thanks, I did."

"Good. They still haven't found the body of the last person who missed a School of Social Sciences meeting."

Williams laughed and said, "Yeah, it's never a good idea to do that." And especially this one, he thought as he picked up his mail and went back to his office. This new center could be a good thing for Tilton in some ways, but for the faculty? He wasn't so sure.

When Williams got to his office, he saw the message light flashing on his phone. He picked up the phone and punched in his message code – two messages. The first was Jered Carr asking him to call back. It didn't sound urgent – just that Jered had been to the Cobbs Creek Second Chance center and wanted to give Joel an update. He decided to wait until this evening to return Jered's call.

The second message was from Ben Peterson asking him to call back when he could. Since he still had five more minutes before he was due in class, Joel decided to call Ben back right away.

"Ben? Joel Williams, how are you?'

"I'm good. Thanks for calling back."

"No problem. What's up?"

"I'm going through some of the information we got from Second Chance about their track record, their attendance and so on. It all looks good, but I don't have anything to check it against. I'd be more comfortable with a way to check what the school gave us against some other source of information."

"I see your point. That would give our numbers a little more reliability."

"Exactly."

"Well, maybe someone in the city government could help. From what I was reading online last night, the City of Philadelphia has a contract with Second Chance to provide an alternative to juvenile imprisonment. Maybe whoever in the city handles that contract could point you in the right direction."

"Hey, that's a good idea. Thanks."

"Let me know what you find out, OK?'

"Will do. Talk to you soon."

"All right."

With the conversation ended, Williams picked up the material he needed for his Current Issues in Criminal Justice class. They were beginning work on their final projects, and he wanted to get ready for them.

For his part, Peterson decided to take Williams' advice. He found the numbers for several city government departments online. After a few minutes of being transferred from one office to another, he was finally connected with Therese Vaughan, who managed the city's alternative-education contracts. After he'd explained to her who he was and what the research team needed, she agreed to meet with him the next day and share some of the city's data.

At six o'clock that evening, Jered Carr pulled into his driveway. He could see that Lauren wasn't home yet, but that didn't surprise him; she had to drive from Valley Forge to Horsham on the Pennsylvania Turnpike, and that could take a long time at rush hour. He got the mail, flipping through the letters and bills as he walked towards the house. When he got inside, Jered went to the refrigerator, pulled out a beer and made his way into the living room, where he sat down on the sofa and began to read through everything. Fifteen minutes later, he heard Lauren's car pull up. A few moments after that, he heard the familiar sound of her heels tapping up the stairs to the door.

"In the living room," he called out when she came inside.

"How was your day?" Lauren asked as she joined her husband.

"Kind of weird, actually. Mind if I sound you out on something?"

"OK."

"Remember last night I mentioned Curtis Templeton to you?"

"Sure."

"You don't know anything more about that, do you?"

"Not any more than I told you yesterday. Curtis Templeton managed to sneak out, found his way to that construction site, climbed up and lost his balance."

"You don't know how he got out or anything?"

"Not for sure. I'm guessing he found a way to sign out without getting caught, but I don't know for a fact. Why?"

"Well, I went to Cobbs Creek today and talked to Sheldon Adler – you know him, right? He basically said that Curtis Templeton was a defiant kid who found a way to sneak out and then had a terrible accident."

"Right. That's what I understand, too. It doesn't sound like you take his word for it, though."

"I'm not sure. There's no reason he should lie, but you know the strict supervision they have at the centers. How could Curtis have gotten out without somebody knowing?"

"I don't know. Teenagers figure things out. Didn't you ever sneak out at night?"

"That's different. I didn't live at a center like Second Chance. I just don't get it."

"I honestly don't get it, either. The reports that came to headquarters didn't really say exactly how he managed it."

[55]

Jered looked up eagerly. "Do you think you could get those reports? Does headquarters still have them?"

"I don't know, Jered. I saw some stuff right after Curtis Templeton's death, but I haven't seen anything in a while. And if there is anything, it's not going to be really accessible."

"Well, could you at least look around?"

"I can't go poking around people's computers. I'd lose my job. And I doubt there'd be anything public."

"You're right, of course. You can't get into people's computers. But could you keep your eyes open? Maybe something'll jump out at you."

"I guess so," Lauren said reluctantly. She was not eager to risk her job.

"Thanks," Jered smiled.

He was silent for a moment. Then, after staring straight ahead of him as he thought, Jered looked up quickly and said, "Of *course*! The parents! Maybe we could interview them. Hon, do you think you could find out their contact information? Maybe help me see if we could get permission to talk to them?"

"I'm not sure their information is on file any more."

"Well, could you at least check?"

"Yeah, sure."

"That'd be really helpful. Thanks," Jered said as he rose from the couch.

Lauren wasn't at all sure she wanted to go looking for what could be confidential information and she didn't much like the sound of Jered's idea. But she did want to support his work if she could. Besides, although it had never occurred to her before, it did seem strange that Curtis Templeton had been able to leave the school building with all of the security measures the school took. Still, she was a little nervous, so for the moment, she decided to change the subject. "Oh, speaking of work, I found out that we've been invited to an Information Night for investors."

"You mean investors for Second Chance, right?"

"Right. They're putting together a whole dinner and presentation thing at the Riverton Hotel, and they want some of the staff to go, too, including me."

"When is it?"

"Next Tuesday night."

"It sounds like it could be a good time."

"Well, I don't know about that. It's the first one I've been invited to, actually. Usually it's just the top people, but this year, they want some of the regular staff, too. Anyway, I hear there's an open bar and lots of food."

"Sounds good to me. Maybe we could even stay overnight and save the drive back."

"OK, I'll make a reservation."

"Thanks."

Lauren smiled and went into the kitchen to figure out what to do about dinner.

The dinner dishes had been cleared away and Jered was flipping through the papers he'd gotten from the Second Chance center when his telephone rang. When he saw Joel Williams' name flash up on the screen, he said,

"Hey, there, Joel, how did you know I was about to call you?"

"Sorry I didn't get to talk to you earlier today. I hope you don't mind my calling you at this hour."

"Not a problem. I was actually hoping you would. I had an interesting visit to Second Chance today and want to talk to you about it."

"OK, shoot."

"Well, I talked to Sheldon Adler, the assistant director of the center. He gave me some useful stuff about the center's policies. Apparently, the students aren't supposed to leave the building without signing in and out, and they can't do that without an adult. So, if Curtis Templeton left the building, somebody would have had to sign him out. And the windows and doors are alarmed. It would have been pretty hard for him to get out that way without a lot of knowledge or some help."

"So, you're saying you think someone at that center knew that Curtis Templeton was AWOL?"

"Could be."

"Unless he forged a name on the sign-out sheet or something."

"Well, there's always that. Kids can be pretty inventive. But…."

"–You think there's more to it than that, right?"

"I don't know, Joel. It's just that I've seen a lot of these kinds of situations. Somebody usually knows what's going on. It might be another student, or a teacher, or a secretary, but somebody usually knows something. That center's got some pretty good supervision policies in place, but somehow, Curtis slipped through the cracks. I find it hard to believe that nobody has any idea how it happened, that's all."

"I know what you're saying, Jered. Well, I'm planning to go up to Philadelphia in a couple of days anyway to interview some of the young people who've finished the Second Chance program. I can see what they have to say."

"I like that idea. And don't you know a few people on the police force there?"

Williams was silent for a moment. "Yeah, of course. I know a guy on the force who used to be a cop here in Tilton. I can try to talk to him, too. He may remember something or have heard something."

"Sounds like a plan."

With the conversation behind him, Williams tapped his fingers reflectively on the edge of the living room coffee table where he'd set the phone. Jered had a point that there was usually somebody who knew something about what a kid was doing. You just had to find out who that somebody was. That might not be easy, but maybe one of the young people he was planning to interview had known Curtis Templeton. That would be a start, anyway. And he'd try to get hold of Carter Barclay, too; he hadn't seen him in a couple of years, but they'd been friends when both had been on the Tilton police force. Barclay had moved to Philadelphia and now worked in the 19th District, which included Cobbs Creek. Maybe he'd know something.

Williams stood up, stretched, and looked ruefully at the large pile of student papers lying next to the telephone. He'd meant to get to those papers earlier in the day, but they were still waiting for him. Well, they'd wait a few more minutes while he took his friendly brown mutt, Oscar, for a quick walk. He needed to clear his head, anyway. He summoned Oscar with a soft whistle, leashed the dog up and the two were soon making their usual round of the neighborhood.

Ben Peterson tossed his trash into the dumpster outside his apartment building. He brushed his hands against the jeans he was wearing and headed back inside. When he got there, he pulled off his Phillies cap and flipped it onto the worn black faux-leather sofa in his living room. Then he sat down on the sofa and picked up his plans for the next day's classes. He'd left the notes there to remind himself that he still needed to work on them. They wouldn't be his best, but he hadn't really been able to keep his mind on what he was doing. Ben's teaching had never been as strong as his data collection and analysis skills. He knew he ought to work on his teaching more, and he was hoping that that seminar he was going to attend would help. But for now, he wasn't nearly as interested in his lesson plans as he was in this whole Curtis Templeton case, if that's what it was. Usually, the soft background noise of the television helped Ben focus on his lessons, but at the moment, he found the all-news channel only irritated him. Tossing his lesson notes behind him onto the sofa, Ben snapped the TV off and began to pace around the living room. Pacing always helped him think more clearly.

Ben knew that statistics only told so much of what was really going on, but in this case, it just seemed odd. Here was a school that hadn't seemed to have any problems with the local police (but he'd ask Joel Williams to check with any contacts he might have about that), and where all the data he had showed the program was successful. Maybe Curtis was just extraordinarily troubled. He knew the team wasn't going to get anywhere until they found out more. Ben wasn't as good with people as Joel and Jered were, so he was going to have to rely on them to get some information about Curtis if they could. All he was sure of was that what happened to the boy just didn't seem to fit with what he'd found out about the school. From what he'd learned, a big part of Second Chance's success came from close supervision of students and lots of student/staff interaction. That was one of their fundamental principles, so it just didn't make sense that nobody would know how a student had managed to leave the school grounds without being seen.

Idle speculation wasn't going to help Ben very much. For now, he'd look at some of the numbers he'd gotten from his Internet search earlier in the day. He returned to the sofa, glanced at the pile of lesson notes he'd left there and then opened the tote he'd used to bring home his printouts. Papers in hand, Ben walked absently to the desktop computer in the alcove next to his kitchen. He hadn't taken an expensive apartment after his divorce – there was no need for that. But he'd paid a considerable amount for a state-of-the-art computer system. His computer had top speed and functionality, and he'd installed cutting-edge applications so that he could do just the kind of heavy-duty data analysis he was planning to do with this Second Chance information.

As he began to look through the information he had, Ben realized that he didn't have complete attendance and grades information on the students. Maybe if he got some more detailed information than he had, he'd be able to figure out what happened to Curtis Templeton. Besides, he and the team would need that data anyway, to look at student achievement in the program. He made a note to find out who at Second Chance would have that much detail, and then turned back to the information he had. The lesson plans would have to wait.

Chapter Three

At six-fifteen the next morning, Joel Williams opened his kitchen door and let Oscar out. He could already see the first hint of sunrise. It was going to be a clear day, and he really ought to go for a run. Besides, he'd be driving into Philadelphia a little later and that would involve a lot of sitting. A run first would be a good idea. So, when Oscar was finished outdoors, Williams whistled for him and fed him when he came trotting back in. Then, Williams laced up his sneakers, slipped on a sweatshirt over his sweatpants and t-shirt and headed out. He set a comfortable pace for himself and soon, the rhythm of his feet slapping the pavement cleared his mind, and he started focusing on what he planned to accomplish with his trip.

At seven o'clock, Lauren Carr slipped her shoes on and picked up her purse and briefcase. She was hoping to get out of the house quietly, without waking Jered. He didn't usually go to the office on Thursday mornings, since he preferred to save the drive time and write at home.

[66]

Lauren had just about reached the door to the garage when she heard Jered's voice.

"Hon, you still here?"

Lauren answered, "Yeah, but I'm just about to leave. Sorry if I woke you."

"You didn't." Jered came around the corner into view. "Can you get me that information about Curtis Templeton's parents?"

"'I'm a little concerned about it, Jered. You know a lot of that stuff's confidential."

"Look, I'm not asking for their Social Security numbers. I really would like to talk to them, though."

"OK, I'll ask my bosses – see what they say. I just want to run it by them and make sure I'm not risking my job."

"Fair enough – and thanks." Jered kissed his wife lightly and watched her leave, enjoying the view as he always did. Then, he went into the kitchen to make some tea and read the paper before he got busy with work.

An hour and a half later, Jered had showered and dressed and was now in his home office, polishing up a paper he planned to submit to *Criminal Justice Quarterly*. He'd finished with the first few pages when his telephone rang. He glanced down at the screen; it was Ben Peterson.

"Hi, Ben, how's it going?"

"I'm good, thanks. You?"

"Good, thanks."

"Listen, I'm putting together some of these charts and other information for our paper, but I don't have names or contact information for Curtis Templeton's family. Do you know their names or anything?"

"I don't, myself. I asked Lauren if she could get them for me. She said she was going to check with her bosses and make sure it was OK and then get back to me."

"I guess that makes sense. I just wanted to have it as background, so if we have to, we can probably do all right without it."

"All right. Well, as soon as I hear from Lauren, I'll let you know."

"Sounds good."

The two men ended their conversation and Jered returned to editing his paper.

Ben put his telephone down and turned back to his computer screen. He was hoping to put some more of this report together today, but for now, he had to go to class. He minimized the document, locked his computer, picked up his papers and notes for class, and left his office, locking the door behind him. After a short walk down the hall and around the corner, Ben came to the classroom where his Introduction to Computer Crimes class was waiting. Fortunately, it was a class he didn't mind too much, so the hour passed quickly.

When class was over, Ben answered a few student questions and returned to his office. He'd just laid his papers and books on his desk when his telephone rang. Jered was calling back.

"Hi, Jered." Ben swung his office chair to the left and sat down.

"Hey, Ben. I just heard from Lauren. She got the clearance for us to interview some parents."

"Oh, that's great! Do you have contact information?"

"Yeah, I got names and so on for twelve families."

"Good. Did you by any chance get contact information for Curtis Templeton's family?"

"Sure did. You're thinking the same thing I am, aren't you?"

"I guess I just think they can give us insights, maybe, that we won't be able to get at the school."

"Exactly."

"Listen, Jered, I'm not really good at this interview stuff. Would you mind doing the interview? You're better at dealing with this kind of thing than I am. Besides, I'm going into center city in a little while to meet with Therese Vaughan from the city government. She's going to give me some of what they have on Second Chance."

"That makes sense. Yeah, I can do that," Jered said.

"Thanks. Talk to you soon."

"OK."

Jered wasn't exactly sure what he was going to say to Curtis' parents, assuming they were even willing to talk to him. What do you say to parents who've lost a child? But it did make sense to talk to them. They'd have insight into their son that possibly nobody else would. Jered had learned over the years that when he worked with parents, he often got some surprisingly useful information about their children. Even when the parents didn't co-operate or were completely dysfunctional, that gave him useful information, too.

Joel Williams looked at the map on his computer screen one more time. As often as he'd been to Philadelphia, he still didn't want to get lost. He was actually looking forward to the interview session he was going to have today. Five former Second Chance students had agreed to meet with him at the First Church of Light, not far from the Cobbs Creek Second Chance Center. Williams knew that five interviews wouldn't give enough information to draw any real conclusions. But he, Jered and Ben had gotten plenty of questionnaire data from other former students. These interviews would mostly be used for anecdotal information on the program. And of course, if one of the interviewees said something worth pursuing, the team could always look into it.

Once Williams felt confident that he knew where he was going, he closed the map and shut down his computer. Then, he picked up his briefcase, lifted his blazer – carefully, this time – from its hook on the back of his office door, and left the office. He went down the hall towards the main departmental office and got his mail from its slot. Seeing nothing important waiting for him, Williams slipped the memos into his briefcase and told Noelle Sanders that he'd be gone for the rest of the day. He was on his way out of the main office when he saw Shirley Mizzello coming in the opposite direction.

"Joel! Just the guy I wanted to see," she called.

"Hi, Shirley."

"Got time for a cup of coffee?"

"I'm really sorry, but I don't. I'm doing a research day trip, and I should already be on my way."

Mizzello's cheerful smile dimmed. "Got it. All right, but please, let's talk tomorrow, OK? It's important."

"Promise."

Williams headed out to Carlton Hall's parking lot where, miraculously, he'd found a parking space close to the building. He settled into his Dodge, turned on the all-sports radio station he liked, and was soon on his way to Philadelphia.

Jered Carr tucked the piece of paper with Curtis Templeton's parents' address into his pocket. Curtis' family had moved away from Cobbs Creek after his death, but they were still in Philadelphia, so Jered set off from Horsham and headed south towards Belmont, where the family now lived. The traffic was heavy, so it took him longer than he'd expected, but he finally got to the right street. He parked his Chevy, and glanced at the number on the house, to be sure it was the right one. He drew a long breath, got out of the car, and headed for the door. This was going to be a difficult conversation and he wasn't looking forward to it at all. He'd thought about calling ahead of time to at least soften the blow but in the end, he'd decided against it. If they knew he was coming, they might not talk to him. He didn't want to risk their not being there.

A tall, dignified-looking woman with her hair pulled back into a short ponytail answered the door. "Excuse me," Jered said, "Are you Shanita Finley?"

"Yeah, that's me," the woman said answered. Her eyes narrowed, and she stood firmly blocking the doorway.

"I'm sorry to just drop in on you like this. My name's Jered Carr; I'm part of a research team doing a study on the Second Chance program. If you have a few minutes, I'd like to talk to you and your husband about the program."

"My husband's not home."

"I understand. I'd really appreciate talking to you, though, if you have a few minutes."

"You with Second Chance?"

"No, I'm not part of Second Chance. I'm a professor at Delaware River University. I'm on a team of people doing a study of the program. That's why I'm hoping to talk to you."

"I don't know what I can tell you."

"Your son, Curtis, was at Second Chance of Cobbs Creek, wasn't he?"

Shanita Finley seemed to gather her thoughts for a moment. Then she said, "You better come in."

She stepped aside and Carr passed her and went into the narrow foyer behind her. She gestured with a hand towards the small living room to the right of the foyer, and the two were soon seated in it. After a moment or so of silence, Carr decided she was waiting for him to start the conversation, so he said, "I know you don't know me and it doesn't change things, but I am truly sorry for the loss of your son." Shanita Finley nodded a stony-faced acknowledgement. Then, Carr continued, "We – my team and I – have gotten lots of material about Second Chance. You know, graduation rates, that kind of thing. In fact, that's how we found out about Curtis. But we also want the opinions of the students and their families."

"You know what happened to my Curtis?"

"I do, and I am sorry. But that's why I wanted to talk to you, if you're willing. We want all kinds of viewpoints on the program. Can you tell me what Curtis thought of it? How he did there?"

"My Curtis, he was a good boy. I'm not saying he was perfect. He started running with some bad people and got in trouble. But he wasn't a bad boy. He wasn't in no gang, neither. He just did some stupid things. When they caught him with that stuff he took from Value Center, the judge put him in Second Chance instead of juvie."

"And how did he do there?"

"He was doing good. He didn't like all the rules, but he was doing good."

"Did he get in trouble while he was there?"

"He got into it once or twice with some of the teachers. He didn't like the way they talked to him sometimes. Like I said, he wasn't perfect. Sometimes he got too bold."

"Ms. Finley, I'm going to get right to the point. How do you think Curtis ended up at that construction site?"

"I don't know. He just snuck out, I guess. Used to do that sometimes when he lived with me, too."

"Do you think Curtis found a way to get out of the building and just left?"

"He must have. My Curtis was a good boy, but he got bored. He liked to go off sometimes."

"And you don't think the school was at fault?"

Shanita Finley's face closed. She sat silently for a moment, then said, "Nobody at that school told my boy to leave the school or go up on that beam. He took a chance."

Carr was surprised at her response. He'd expected her to be upset with the school, to want to blame someone there. In his experience, a lot of parents wanted to blame the school, or the system, or a teacher, or another child for their children's dangerous or illegal choices. This woman didn't seem to feel that way. Carr decided to be careful; he didn't want to stir up resentment where there was none. Besides, he didn't want to be guilty of influencing an interviewee's responses. He chose his words carefully, "I liked some of what I saw at the school when the team and I were there."

"It's better than juvie." Shanita glanced at the clock on top of the television and then said, "I'm sorry, but I got to get ready for work. I work second shift and I got to pick up my kids at school and drop them off at my cousin's on the way."

"I understand. I appreciate that you took the time to talk to me. I wonder," Carr decided to take a risk, "whether you'd be willing to meet with our team again?"

After a long pause, she said, "I got my job, I got my kids, I don't have time to go somewhere and meet with somebody. And I met with enough people already about Curtis. No need me saying nothing else."

"Well, if you change your mind –"

"– Look, Mr. Carr. I got nothing against you. I'm just done talking about this whole thing, OK? Now I got to get ready for work."

Jered took his cue. He didn't want to antagonize his hostess, and he could see that she wasn't willing to say anything more. He nodded, and said, "I'll let you get to it, then. Thanks for your time."

After they'd said goodbye, Carr returned to his Chevy and headed back north towards Horsham and home. He wasn't sure quite how to take Shanita Finley's reaction to his questions. She'd been polite enough, and he supposed it made sense that she'd be sick of talking about her son's death. He'd never lost a child and couldn't imagine what it must be like. Maybe wanting to forget the whole thing was a natural reaction. But he couldn't shake the feeling that there was more she could have told him.

Shanita Finley watched Carr leave. Then she slowly climbed the stairs to the second floor of the row house. She hadn't expected Curtis' death to come up like this again. She hadn't been prepared. Well, she'd done the best she could. And as she thought about the conversation she'd just had, she figured she'd done pretty well, especially with being surprised like that. No, she couldn't think of anything else she would have said, even if she'd had time.

Ben Peterson arrived at the City of Philadelphia's Municipal Services Building five minutes before he was supposed to meet with Therese Vaughan. The drive north from New Castle hadn't been too difficult, but he'd had to drive around for a few minutes looking for a place to park. Luckily, it wasn't raining, although the day had clouded up somewhat, so he hadn't much minded having to park three blocks away. When he got into the building, he took the elevator to the 13th floor, where the city's finance offices were located. After a bit of wandering around, he found the right office. He tapped on the frame of the open office door and

Therese Vaughan looked up from her computer. She was a heavyset woman with her black hair cut neatly in a medium-length bob.

"Can I help you?"

"Yes, thanks. I'm Ben Peterson. We spoke on the phone yesterday."

"Right, of course. You're the one who's doing the study on the Second Chance program, aren't you?"

"That's right."

"OK, come on in and have a seat. What can I do for you?"

Ben sat down in the chair opposite Therese's desk chair. "What I'm really looking for, I think, is any information your office might have about Second Chance."

"Do you mean their original contract?"

"That'd be a good start. But I also mean attendance, grades, annual reviews, anything like that."

"Second Chance submits attendance data at the beginning of each year, and grades data at the end of each year. Is that what you mean?"

"Exactly. What I basically want is an outside source of information on the program – something I can compare to their own records."

"I see. Any particular years you need?"

"The last four or five if you have them."

"We just got this year's data and we're still going over it, so it's not available yet. But I can give you some other years."

"Thanks, I'd really appreciate it."

"Just give me a couple of minutes. I have to look up the files."

"Take your time. I'm not in a hurry."

Therese nodded and got up from her desk. She crossed her office and opened the second drawer of a large filing cabinet. After a few minutes of flipping through file folders, she found what she was looking for. "Here's the original contract," she said.

She passed the contract to Ben, and then returned to her desk where she began to search for what she wanted on her computer. After a few moments, she looked up with a satisfied smile. "Here it is. Just let me print it out for you."

"Thanks."

After a few mouse clicks, the attendance data had been printed, and Therese handed it to Ben. He thanked her and flipped through the documents.

"It looks like everything's here except this year's form. And you said you'll get that in a few weeks, right?"

"Right."

"Could you let me know when you get that information? That way, I can cross-reference it with what I have."

"Sure, no problem."

Ben took another look at the forms, thanked Therese for her time, and left her office. His next step would be to try to get detailed attendance information from the Cobbs Creek Center.

When Ben had left Therese's office, she glanced quickly at her watch. It was nearly noon. She would have to leave if she was going to be on time for her weekly twelve-thirty meeting with her daughter Nicole's teacher. Nine-year-old Nicole had been diagnosed with Asperger's Syndrome and attended a private program for children on the spectrum of developmental disorders. She'd been doing well, there, too. Her teacher had been working hard with her on recognizing people's moods and responding appropriately, so Nicole was much better than she had been at picking up on social cues. She was making progress in some other areas, too – more than she had in her public-school-funded program. Therese was glad she'd found this program, but it was outrageously expensive. She had good insurance coverage as a city employee, but it didn't cover private programs like this one. Still, Nicole was doing so well that Therese felt she had no choice but to do whatever it took to pay Nicole's tuition and other fees. She felt lucky she'd found a way to deal with Nicole's expenses.

Chapter Four

Joel Williams pulled into the parking lot of the First Church of Light. The traffic into the city had been heavy, so he was glad that he'd allowed plenty of time. He got out of the car, picked up his briefcase and, after locking the car, headed towards the building. When he got there, Williams saw a sign directing him to the social hall. He turned right instead of heading into the locked church building itself, and was soon at the door of the social hall. When he went in, he saw five expectant faces turned towards him. After a moment, one of the people in the group, a tall young man with a self-conscious smile, got up from the table where the group was sitting and came towards him.

"Are you Mr. Williams?"

"That's me."

"I'm Rondell Harrison. You called us about meeting here."

"I sure did. And thanks for your time. Thanks to the rest of you, too," Williams said, nodding to the other people at the table. Then, glancing around him, he said, "This was a good idea for a place to meet."

Rondell answered, "My mom, she's the secretary here at the church. So they said we could use the hall."

"Good thinking."

Williams sat down at the table and placed his briefcase next to him. Then, he looked around at the group and said, "I really appreciate all of you meeting me here. I'm hoping you'll give me some useful information about Second Chance. But first, we've only talked on the phone, so I'd like to put faces with voices. I've met you, Rondell, but how about the rest of you?"

"Kiana"

"David"

"Marisol"

"Sandra"

"Thanks," Williams said. He felt lucky that there were only five young people here; it would be easier to remember their names. Once he'd glanced at the group again and begun to associate names with faces, he said, "OK, maybe you can tell me something about Second Chance."

"What do you want to know?" This came from Kiana, the young woman who sat to Williams' left.

"I'd like to know what your experiences at Second Chance were like."

"You mean did we like it there?"

"We can start with that."

"Well, for me, it was a good place. Home sucked, so it was better for me to live there."

"What about your classes?"

"Yeah, I took classes," Kiana said. "I got my diploma."

"What are your plans now?"

Kiana glanced down at her slightly swollen belly and said, "Me and my boyfriend are getting married. He works in his dad's garage and we're going to live with his parents till the baby comes."

"I graduated, too," Rondell said. "I'm going into the army next month."

"That's great," Williams said. "What about the rest of you?"

Sandra said, "I'm going to start at community college in January. I want to be a dental assistant."

"Me, I'm working in my uncle's store. As soon as I save up enough, I'm getting an apartment," David said.

"What about you, Marisol?" Williams asked.

"I'm going to go to culinary school. Maybe even have my own restaurant someday."

"It sounds like all of you are working on getting your lives together," Williams said. "I give you a lot of credit for that. Do you think being at Second Chance helped you?"

"It helped me," Rondell said. "I would have ended up in prison if I hadn't been sent there."

"Me, too," Sandra said. The other three nodded their agreement.

"What about life there?" Williams continued.

"What's it like at the school?'

"They got a lot of rules," David said, "I didn't like that. But it's better than juvie."

Kiana added, "The teachers, most of them work real hard."

"The food is bad!" This comment from Marisol brought a burst of knowing laughter from the others. Williams grinned, too.

"Anything else you didn't like about Second Chance?" he asked.

The former students looked at each other. "I don't know. Every place got problems," said Sandra.

"Good point," said Williams. "Anything in particular you're thinking of?"

"You gotta share rooms. Sometimes I didn't get along with my roommate," David said.

"You can't do what you want to do. They got schedules there, and they tell you what to do," Marisol said.

Williams made notes on a notepad he'd pulled out of his briefcase, and then asked them a few more questions about the classes they'd taken. Then, once he'd sensed that the young people had begun to relax, he edged closer to the topic that really interested him. "Did you guys know a kid named Curtis Templeton?"

Again, the group looked at one another. Finally, David said, "You mean the kid that got killed at the construction site"

"That's the one."

"I had a class with him. English."

"Were you friends?"

"I mean, we hung out sometimes. He was OK."

Williams looked expectantly at the others. Rondell said, "I didn't know him real well, but I didn't have a problem with him."

Sandra and Kiana looked at each other, and then Sandra said, "He wasn't always OK."

"What do you mean?" Williams asked. A second later, he realized he'd reacted too quickly. Sandra looked down and said, "Nothing. I didn't mean nothing."

Williams thought for a moment, mentally crossed his fingers, and then said, "Look, I'm not a cop or anything. It's just that when I find out a kid died, I guess I can't help wanting to know what happened. What kind of kid he was. I'm not interested in getting anybody in trouble. Your names aren't going to be mentioned in anything I write."

There was a long silence. Then Kiana said, "Curtis wasn't evil or anything, but he had a big mouth. Got on people's last nerve sometimes."

"Yeah," David said. "He found out stuff, too, like if you had cigarettes or something."

"What did he do if he found something out?" Williams asked, reminding himself not to push too hard.

"Depends what he found out and if he liked you. If he liked you, he didn't do nothing, especially if you gave him something, like cigarettes or whatever," David replied.

Williams waited a moment, then said, "Sounds like he could be a pain if he didn't like you."

"If he didn't like you, you had to be real careful or he'd get you in big trouble. No privileges, no nothing." This came from Sandra.

Williams was beginning to get a picture of the kind of person Curtis Templeton was. He was also beginning to see how Curtis had managed to sneak out of the school. If he was the kind who found things out and collected favors in return, he could have found a way to slip out and be covered. Still aware that this was a delicate conversation, Williams said, "I wonder if that's how Curtis managed to sneak out that day."

Rondell took the cue. "You mean he got some help from somebody he knew something about?"

"That kind of thing, yeah."

The young people looked at one another. For a moment, everyone thought about it. Then, slowly, David said, "I guess so. I mean, I didn't help him, but he couldn't have gotten out just by himself. But he worked in the office. That was his job. He might have figured out some way to get out."

"His job?"

"Yeah, everybody at the center got jobs. You clean, or you work in the office, or you do something," Sandra said. "Curtis worked in the office. You know, he made copies and filed and did things like that."

William took in this new information. A kid who worked at the school's office. Who found out things and sometimes used those things to get what he wanted. Someone who could be trouble if he didn't get what he wanted.

After a short time, Sandra said, "I don't know. Like I said, Curtis worked in the office. Could have been a lot of people he knew stuff about."

"Nobody in particular you can think of?"

"No," Kiana said, "Nobody I know of for sure."

"Me, either," said Rondell.

"It's OK. I appreciate what you have told me," said Williams.

After a few more minutes of conversation and a few more details about Second Chance, Williams took his leave of the group. He was hoping that Jered had gotten some useful information from Curtis Templeton's parents. Then they might be able to get a better picture of what Curtis had really been like. There seemed to be something more going on here than just a boy falling off of some scaffolding. Well, no use keeping these young people here any longer. They'd just get nervous, and besides, he had their contact information. After repeating his thanks, Williams stood up, picked up his briefcase and headed back towards the car.

He'd almost reached the car when he heard a voice behind him.

"Hey, Mister."

Williams turned around and looked into Marisol's troubled dark eyes.

"About Curtis? That boy you were asking about?"

Williams nodded, "Something you remembered?"

"Do you know something about what happened to Curtis? That why you're asking questions?"

"I wish I knew more. That's why I'm asking."

Williams waited to see if she would say anything more.

Marisol swallowed hard. "It's just – me and Curtis were together, you know? We never told nobody. We just didn't want to hear about it from everybody. Wasn't their business. But, well, you know…"

"I think I do. Must have been hard on you."

Marisol blinked, looked away, and then back at Williams. "Yeah, well, whatever. It's over now, right?"

"Maybe not. Do you remember anything strange happening right before Curtis died?"

Marisol's brows wrinkled as she thought. "Yeah. I mean, Curtis, he was talking kind of weird the day before it happened."

"That right? You remember what he said?"

"He just kept talking about he didn't get it and it didn't make sense."

"Did he tell you anything else?"

"Nope."

"Did anything happen that day that might have been confusing?"

"Nothing happened to me. I don't know about Curtis."

"Nothing weird happened at the school?"

"I don't think so. I mean, we had classes, we ate, we did our jobs. You know, same as always."

"And nobody came to the school? I mean somebody who wasn't a student or a parent?"

"Not that I know about. That was a long time ago, though."

"I know. It's hard to remember. Did you tell any of this to the police when it happened?"

"You crazy? You live around here, you don't talk to the police."

"Right, of course. Well, I'm glad you told me. It might help me get some answers."

Marisol relaxed a bit. Then, she said, "You think maybe someone killed Curtis?"

"I don't know. If there's anything else you want to tell me, though…"

"You gonna talk to the cops?"

Williams didn't want to lie. "I will probably say something about this to a friend of mine who's a cop in the 19th. But I won't use your name."

Marisol looked at Williams for a long moment. Then she nodded and said, "I gotta go." A minute later, she'd disappeared back into the building.

Jered Carr sat staring blankly at the wide-screen TV at Scotty's Den, a bar about a mile from home. He took occasional absent-minded sips of the beer he'd ordered as he watched the football game. He was trying to make sense of Shanita Finley. There was a break in the action of the game, and the local news announcer came on to highlight the evening's top stories.

…and in Philadelphia today, Superior Court Judge Roger Warren issued a gag order in the Mob trial of Johnny Gianatti, who's been charged with racketeering, money laundering and tax evasion…

Of course! A gag order! What if Shanita Finley was keeping quiet because she'd agreed to? That made sense. Jered slowly nodded to himself as he thought that through. Somebody wanted Curtis Templeton's death to be kept as low-key as possible. That was logical, too. Programs like Second Chance wouldn't last long if they got a reputation for being lax, especially about supervision. Jered was sure that Curtis' mother could tell him more if she wanted to. He would see what Lauren had to say about it. He finished his beer, put some money in the tip jar near the cash register and left.

Ten minutes later, Lauren heard the sound of Jered's Chevy pulling into their driveway. She wondered where he'd been, since Thursday was usually his day to work at home. Well, she'd find out soon enough. He sometimes did stop into the office if he needed a book or to meet with someone. "Hi," she turned and smiled as he came into the kitchen.
"Hi. How was your day?"
"Not bad. Yours?"

"Well, I met with Curtis Templeton's mother today."

"That must have been hard. I can't imagine what she must have gone through."

"Neither can I. Funny thing is, I thought for sure she'd blame the school. A lot of parents do. But she didn't. She basically said that her son took a risk. Don't you think that's weird?"

"I don't know. I know what you're saying, but it's hard to know how a parent would react. Maybe that's her way of dealing with everything."

"Maybe. It seems odd, though. I'm wondering if maybe the reason is that she's deliberately keeping her mouth shut."

Lauren was quick to catch his point. "You mean somebody might be paying her or something? Isn't that a little far-fetched?"

"Could be. And I don't know what it's like to be a parent. I don't know what I'd be like. But I keep having the feeling I would want to blame somebody – anybody."

"I probably would, too."

After a moment, Jered asked, "Lauren, do you think someone at Second Chance might be paying her?"

"You mean somebody at headquarters?" Lauren asked. She sat down slowly at the kitchen table. "Jered, I don't even want think about that. I work with those people. I don't want to think any of them would pay somebody to keep quiet."

"I don't want to, either, but do you think it's possible?"

"That's the problem." Lauren looked down and bit her bottom lip. "I can't swear it isn't possible. I haven't heard anything, but that doesn't mean it couldn't have happened."

"Well, did Shanita Finley ever go to headquarters? Did she ever meet with anyone there?"

Lauren thought briefly. "She and, I guess, her husband came up right after Curtis died. I didn't really meet with them, though. They met with the company president and with Mark Donnelly, but I wasn't in on those meetings."

Now it was Jered's turn to think. Then he asked, "Do you think you could find out what happened in them?"

"That would be kind of hard. It was two years ago, remember."

"I know. And nobody would keep minutes from that kind of meeting."

"Besides, Jered, this is risky. Even if you're right, I'd have to go looking for the information. I could get in real trouble."

"Look, I don't want you to risk your job or anything. But could you keep your eyes open?"

"That I can do. Oh, and before I forget, I printed out some attendance records for you. I thought they might be helpful."

"Oh, thanks. Those will be really useful. Ben wants to use them to compare with the records he gets from the City of Philadelphia."

Lauren pulled her briefcase across the table towards her and opened it. Glancing quickly through its contents, she pulled out a manila envelope and handed it to her husband. Jered took the envelope, opened it and flipped briefly through the papers in it. "This looks pretty comprehensive. Thanks."

Lauren nodded and then, concern in her voice, said, "Jered, do you really think something might be going on at Second Chance?"

"I don't know. It all seems a little strange, that's all. I hope not, though."

Fifty-two miles away, in New Castle, Delaware, Ben Peterson was having dinner at the Seaside Tavern with Mark Donnelly from Second Chance. The Seaside was out of Ben's usual financial reach, but Mark had insisted that they "eat somewhere nice." Seaside was certainly that. Vaguely Colonial in its décor, the restaurant had dark wood-paneled walls, sconce lighting and a first-class seafood and steak menu. The wine list was impressive, too.

Donnelly had called Peterson that afternoon and suggested getting together for a working dinner, and Ben had agreed, happy for a change from his usual bachelor fare of microwaved food.

"So," Donnelly said, taking a sip of his Pinot Gris, "tell me more about the project. What have you found? I'd really like an update."

"I'm glad you asked, actually," Ben replied. "I have some questions that you might be able to answer for me."

"OK, go ahead."

"Well, to start with, we've found some encouraging things about recidivism and about high school completion. When we looked at students who completed Second Chance versus those who completed other alternative programs, we found that Second Chance graduates were slightly more likely to complete high school and get a diploma. We also found that they were slightly less likely to be arrested again before the age of twenty-one."

"That sounds good."

"We thought so. And young people in Second Chance are far more likely to complete high school than are those who go to prison schools. They're also significantly less likely to be arrested again before the age of twenty-one."

"That sounds even better."

"The bottom line in terms of those factors is that Second Chance seems to have at least some slightly positive effects for students who are involved in the program."

"That's terrific! I'll be really glad to have those numbers to back us up."

"Good. As I said, though, I do have a couple of questions."

"Hopefully I can answer them for you."

"Well, one's about your security procedures."

"You mean data security? Privacy?"

"No, security as in students entering and leaving the building."

"Oh, well, the individual centers can give you the nuts and bolts on that. I do know, though, that students aren't allowed off campus unsupervised. It's policy. They have to be signed out and then only in the company of a staff member or guardian."

"And there's no way around that system?"

"What are you getting at?"

Ben took a bite of his lobster and a sip of his Moselle as he thought about what to say next. Then, his mind made up, he said, "When my team and I were looking at the Second Chance system, we read about the death of Curtis Templeton. It seems that he managed to leave the Cobbs Creek center unsupervised and ended up dead. Before we put our names on a study of the program, we'd like to know what happened to him."

Now it was Donnelly's turn to pause. He glanced out the window for a moment, and then he said, "Yes, of course. I'm not surprised that you'd want to know about Curtis Templeton. A real tragedy."

"It certainly seemed like it. Can you tell me what happened?"

"Well, I wasn't there, of course. I'm at Valley Forge and this happened at Cobbs Creek. But from what I understand, he found a way to sneak out of school one day about two years ago. He went over to a construction site near the school – couldn't resist it. You know how kids are about construction sites. He climbed up on some scaffolding, lost his balance and, well, he fell. It had rained the night before, and the area was probably still slippery."

"What I'm wondering is how he got out."

"Well, I'm not proud to admit it, but we think he found a way to slip out. We did a study of the facilities after Curtis' death, and of course the police did an investigation, too. All of the window and door alarms and so on were working properly, and we did a training session for the staff, so this kind of thing wouldn't happen again. And it hasn't."

"Did you ever find out exactly how he managed it?"

"We've been working on that. But why this sudden interest in this case? Admittedly it was a real shame, but we're talking about one case in the course of a few years of being open. It's not like this is an everyday kind of thing. Does it have to go in your study?"

Ben sensed Donnelly's defensiveness. Quickly, he said, "Oh, I know. Second Chance has a fine record. I guess that's what made us so curious about this one case. It sticks out, if you know what I mean. Besides, if we're going to do an accurate study, we need to have full information about the school – even negative information."

Donnelly decided that it wouldn't make sense to get his back up about the Templeton case. Not right now, anyway. This research team was bound to have found out about the death, and it was logical to ask questions. No, it was better to co-operate and answer Peterson's questions. No good would come from alienating these people. They could be very helpful to Second Chance. If they did a good study, which in Donnelly's mind meant a study that reflected well on the company, Second Chance could get contracts with other cities as well as the one the company had with the School District of Philadelphia.

"Sure, I understand," he finally said. "It wasn't one of our finer moments, and I have to admit I'm not proud to be talking about it, but I can certainly understand why you want to know more. The truth is, we don't know exactly how Curtis Templeton sneaked out. We know he didn't simply walk out. He couldn't have done that because of the alarm system. And we had the walls, floors and basement area checked for any exit he could have used. There was none. But we have very strict policies in place now about escorting students out of the building. Now, not only do they have to be signed out, but the responsible adult has to show ID. There are other precautions, too. We just don't want this sort of thing to happen ever again."

"I'm sure you don't. It was a real tragedy, and I appreciate your telling me what you do know. Is there anyone else who might know something and who'd be willing to talk to us?"

"Hmm… how about if I think about that and then Email you some names? Will that work?"

"Sure, fine. Thanks."

All of a sudden Donnelly snapped his fingers. "I've got it! Next Tuesday there's going to be an Information Night about Second Chance at the Riverton Hotel. It's basically a get-together to attract some investors, if you want to know the truth, but a bunch of our staff will be there. In fact, I think Jered and Lauren Carr are going, and we'd love to have you and Joel Williams, too. It's a nice hotel and you'll have a chance to get to know some of the other Second Chance folks. I can even swing an overnight stay if you'd like – nice little getaway."

"Thanks! I'll talk to Jered and Joel about it."

"Excellent," Mark Donnelly said, smiling broadly. "I think that'll be terrific."

Chapter Five

Detective Carter Barclay was just finishing his second cup of coffee. He'd been working at the 19th District for four years and had finally made the adjustment to working in a big city instead of the small, college town of Tilton. It often meant he got less sleep though, and last night had been no exception. He'd been working an arson case until after one and had clocked back in at seven-thirty this morning. Now, he yawned, drained his coffee and straightened up from his desk to return to the coffee pot. He'd just stood up when his phone rang. Smothering a curse, he picked it up.

"19th District, Barclay," he snapped.

"Carter? That you? It's Joel Williams from Tilton."

"Joel! Good to hear from you! How are you?"

"I'm fine, but it sounds like I caught you at a bad time."

"Oh, no, just not enough sleep. Late-night case last night and then in early this morning."

"The long hours are one thing I don't miss about the force."

"So how are you, Joel? You still at Tilton?"

"Oh, yeah, still in the Criminal Justice department. Doing some research right now, actually, and besides catching up, that's why I'm calling."

"You want my help with some research?"

"I'd sure appreciate it."

"Are you in town?"

"Yeah. I did some work here yesterday and stayed overnight to save the drive back to Tilton."

"OK, then maybe we can get together for lunch or something?"

"Sounds good. How about I meet you at the station and we can go from there. That work?"

"Yup. Twelve-thirty?"

"See you then."

Barclay hung up the phone and smiled. He hadn't seen Williams in a couple of years; it would be good to catch up. But right now he needed more coffee.

Sheldon Adler hung up his office phone and furrowed his brow in an effort to concentrate. Mark Donnelly from headquarters had called that morning to find out how the visit with Jered Carr had gone. Adler didn't think he'd made any mistakes, but you could never tell. The thing that worried him most now was that Carr's visit probably wouldn't be the last. He decided to check his computer files again, just to be sure. He'd be extra-thorough, too, and check the server to be sure there wasn't anything there that shouldn't be there. He got up and closed the door to his office to get at least some measure of privacy. Then he began carefully looking through his hard drive. He'd check the server next.

Ben Peterson walked slowly down the hall from the main office of his department towards his own office. He was so intent on the documents he was looking at that he almost passed his door. Realizing that he wasn't paying attention, he turned just in time, narrowly missing the doorjamb. Jered Carr had just emailed some of Second Chance's attendance and grades information, and Ben wanted to read the printed version. The note that came with the material said that Lauren had gotten the information from headquarters. Ben sat down in his office chair, spread the sheets out and began to look them over. After he'd read everything, he opened up his computer's spreadsheet program and transferred the data Jered had sent.

Ben entered the attendance figures and overall grade averages for the last four years into a new spreadsheet. Then, just to check himself for accuracy, he opened up the spreadsheet document that contained the attendance data from the City of Philadelphia. As he looked at the two sets of numbers, Ben realized that something wasn't right. The data from the city showed more names and attendance records than the data from Second Chance's headquarters did. Muttering to himself, Ben painstakingly went through both spreadsheets again. Still the same difference. It didn't make sense, and he'd checked everything twice.

He leaned back in his chair and thought for a few moments. Then, abruptly, he swung forward and picked up his phone.

"Department of Criminal Justice. Jered Carr."

"Jered, hi, it's Ben. I didn't catch you in the middle of anything, did I?"

"No, I have a meeting with the Curriculum Review Committee, but I've got a few minutes."

"Good. I've just been looking over some of the data from Second Chance again. Thanks for sending it."

"Oh, I'm glad you got it. Were you able to read it all?"

"Yeah, that's not the problem."

"There's a problem?"

"Yeah, here's the thing. The information Lauren gave you is different from what I got from the City."

"Different? How different?"

"The data I got from the City shows more names and different attendance totals."

"That doesn't make sense."

"Not to me, either. I think there must be some kind of entry error or something. I was thinking of going over to Cobbs Creek anyway in a bit. I'll ask over there. I'm sure they have some list or something that I can use to check what I've got."

"That's a good idea."

"By the way, last night I had dinner with Mark Donnelly, and he gave me the impression he really wants us to come up with some positive results."

"Well, I guess that makes sense from his perspective. They want to look good."

"Exactly. And in some ways, they do. I mean, Second Chance students show lower recidivism, higher graduation rates, and on the other measures, too, they do better than the ones who aren't in alternative programs. And they do slightly better than those in other programs."

"It sounds like there's a 'but' in there."

"There is. Curtis Templeton."

Jered sighed. "Yeah, I agree. That's a problem. I went there yesterday and got some information on classes, procedures and so on."

"I know. That's actually why I'm calling. Can you fill me in before I go over there?"

"OK, here's what they told me…"

Jered gave Ben the information Sheldon Adler had given him. When he'd finished, he said, "You know, as I listen to myself, it doesn't sound like a lot of very in-depth stuff."

"Maybe not, but it provides good background. If you don't mind, I'm going to use what you found and ask them for more detail. The more we have on

everything at that school, the better. It might explain
what I found in the attendance data, too."

"Makes sense to me."

"So, you don't mind if I go over the same ground
you did?"

"Another pair of eyes and ears can be helpful.
Besides, I'm not the data analyst that you are."

"All right. And then in a day or so, you and Joel and
I can talk and see where we are."

"OK."

"Oh, and before I forget, Jered, I wanted to ask you,
are you and Lauren going to the Information Night
at Second Chance next Tuesday?"

"Yeah, we'll be there. Will you be going?"

"Yeah, I'm going."

"All right. Look I need to get ready for my meeting.
Talk to you soon, OK?"

"OK."

After finishing his call to Jered, Ben placed a quick
call to the Cobbs Creek center to find out whether
Sheldon Adler was in that day. Told that Adler was
there, he was put through and arranged with Adler
for a meeting early that afternoon. He finished his

call just before he heard the tap on his office door that meant his first advisee of the day had arrived. Fortunately, he only had three appointments scheduled, and none of them turned out to involve anything more than a review and sign-off for his students' Senior Project outlines. Focusing hard to keep his mind on what his advisees were showing him, Ben managed to get through the visits without his students knowing how distracted he was.

As soon as he'd signed off on the last outline, Ben checked his calendar to be sure he didn't have anything else scheduled for that afternoon. Then, he quickly shut down his computer, put some printouts he'd prepared into his satchel and left his office. The sky was beginning to darken, which didn't bode well for the weather this afternoon, so he walked quickly out to the parking lot and got into his Subaru. Within minutes, he was on the highway that led directly to Philadelphia. The drive to the Cobbs Creek section of West Philadelphia took him just under an hour, but at least the traffic wasn't too bad.

When Ben arrived at Second Chance of Cobbs
Creek, he couldn't help but be struck by the
difference between the quiet, old-fashioned,
picturesque neighborhood where he lived in New
Castle and this urban, economically-depressed
working-class neighborhood in West Philadelphia.
Although Ben had lived in the area all his life and
knew that all of the different sections of
Philadelphia were unique, he was still capable of
being startled by the diversity in the city. He hadn't
been to Cobbs Creek very often, though, and as he
glanced up and down the street where the Second
Chance center was located, he thought of the people
who lived in this area and was glad that there were
some options for their children. But that didn't
lessen his concerns about this whole Curtis
Templeton case and, with that in mind, he headed
into the building.

Sheldon Adler stared at his computer screen, trying
to be sure that everything on his hard drive was
organized. The jangling of his office phone made
him nearly jump. "Yes?" he said.

The student receptionist answered, "Mr. Adler, Mr. Ben Peterson is here to see you." With a knot tightening his stomach, Adler said, "OK, thanks, Patrice. I'll be there in just a minute or two. Please ask Mr. Peterson to wait."

"OK," the girl said, and ended the call.

Sheldon took a deep breath and waited until he felt calmer. After a moment or two, he went down to the main office to greet Ben.

"Dr. Peterson? I'm Sheldon Adler. Nice to meet you."

"Nice to meet you, too. And thanks for making time for me."

"Oh, not a problem at all. Let's go down to my office. We can talk there."

"Thanks."

Once the two men were seated in Adler's office, he said, "So what can I do for you?"

"I know my colleague, Jered Carr, was here the other day, and we appreciate all the help you're giving us. I just have a few follow-up questions."

"OK."

"They told me at headquarters that you're the person here who handles things like attendance data and grades and so on. Is that right?"

"That's right."

"As you can guess, part of our study looks at attendance rates, grades and some other indicators of how these young people do. Since you've got the most detailed records for this center, I thought I'd ask to take a look at what you've got."

"Happy to help. What do you need?"

"Well, I'd like to get a look at your attendance records and overall grades for this center."

"You got District approval to get that information, right?"

"Yes, we filled out that paperwork and got the official approval quite some time ago."

"Right, of course. Just checking. Otherwise, I couldn't release anything."

"Oh, I understand."

"If you have a little time, I can print out those records for you."

"I'd appreciate that, and I don't mind waiting."

Adler nodded and turned to his computer screen. "Just give me a minute," he said as he moved his mouse around on its pad. Within a few moments, his printer whirred to life and began churning out paper. After a short while, he'd finished the printing. He stood up, picked up the papers from the printer's tray and handed them to Peterson, who riffled through them.

"This looks terrific. Thanks," Peterson said. Then, after a moment, he frowned and flipped through the papers again.

"Wait a sec. I've got a question for you."

"Sure."

"One reason I wanted to look at this data was to compare it to the attendance data I got from Therese Vaughan at the City of Philadelphia. I wanted a check on myself, too, to make sure I was using the right numbers. These numbers you gave me look like they match the City's."

"That's right. They're supposed to. We send our attendance data over to the City every year."

"That's what Ms. Vaughan told me. But the thing is, I got different attendance numbers from headquarters. Shouldn't those numbers match?"

"You got numbers from headquarters, too? You *are* thorough."

Peterson laughed a little. "Yeah, I like to check everything before I put it in my work. That's why I was wondering about that discrepancy."

"Well, the records I just gave you are the accurate ones. That's why they match the City's numbers. The reason the numbers from headquarters are different is probably that one of our attendance sheets was overlooked by accident when the data got sent up there. That happens every once in a while. That's why you're much better off going with the more updated, accurate numbers I just gave you."

"Got it. Well, I appreciate your giving me this."

"Not a problem. Is there anything else you need?"

"Not right at the moment, thanks. Can I get back to you if something pops up?"

"Sure."

"Thanks."

Adler walked to the door of the school with his guest and, when Peterson had gone, returned to his office. After about ten minutes, he pulled his cell phone out of his pocket and punched in a number. "Hey, it's me. Look, we may have a problem...."

At twelve-twenty, Joel Williams pulled into the parking lot across the street from district headquarters for the 19th District. He got out of his car and locked it, then glanced warily up at the darkening sky. It was beginning to mist, so he walked quickly into the building. When he got to the front desk, he gave his name to the receptionist, who said he would let Barclay know Williams was there. Williams thanked the young man and took a seat in the waiting area.

He hadn't waited for more than five minutes when the door to the waiting area opened and Carter Barclay came forward to greet his old friend. Barclay was thirty-eight years old, tall and slender, with a shaved head. He and Williams shook hands and Barclay said, "Good to see you, Joel!"
"You, too, Carter. It's been too long."
"It has been a while. How've you been?"
"I've been good. How about you?"

"Good. It gets a little crazy around here, and I don't get enough sleep, but nothing new about that. Let's get some food."

"Right behind you."

The two men left the building and within a short time, were seated at Jim's Steaks, a popular nearby steak and hoagie restaurant. They ordered steak sandwiches, fries and drinks, and while they waited for their food, Barclay said, "So tell me how you are."

"I'm doing really well – enjoying being at the university."

"Good. I wondered how you'd like the change. Isn't it a little tame for you?"

"No, not really," Williams smiled to himself.

Just then, a waitress arrived with their lunch, and the next few moments were quiet as the two men began to eat.

"Best cheesesteak in town," Barclay said as he took a sip from his soda.

"You can't get cheesesteaks like this in Tilton," Williams agreed. Then he asked, "So how do you like the 19th?"

"Well, it ain't Tilton, that's for sure," Barclay answered. "I like the people I work with, and I think we're doing good things here. It's just hard sometimes."

"Yeah, from what I've seen, some of the people here are pretty desperate."

"That's just it. That's what they are."

"Ever miss Tilton?"

Barclay thought about it for minute. "Yeah, sometimes. I remember when you and me were partners, and we'd actually have time to stop for a burger when we were on duty."

"Yeah, or a beer at Morley's after shift."

"That place still there?"

"Still there."

"You remember the birthday party we had there for Captain Schneider?"

"Sure do. I think they spent the next two days cleaning up after us."

The two men laughed, and then Barclay said, "Captain Schneider was a good boss."

"I hear he still is."

"So what brings you here, Joel? You said you wanted my help with something."

"I do. I'm working with two other people on a research study. We're doing a study of Second Chance – you know the program I mean? – and I have a couple of questions."

"Second Chance…you mean the alternative school, right?"

"That's the one."

"I don't know how much I can tell you. What, exactly, do you want to know?"

"Well, for starters, what's the school's reputation like? Do the kids do well there? Do they cause trouble?"

"They don't cause any more trouble than any other kids."

"You get a lot of calls from there?"

"We've only been called out there a couple of times that I know about. Once was to get a drunk off the property, and once we were there because a kid at the school died."

"You mean Curtis Templeton?"

"I can't be sure of the name, but that sounds right. Fell off some scaffolding a couple of years ago."

"That's got to be rough on everyone. The school, the parents, everyone."

"Got to be. Don't know what I'd do if my Angelique died. How'd you know about that, anyway?"

"We were doing some background research on the school and the story popped up on a newspaper archive search."

Barclay nodded, "Yeah, it made a couple of the papers."

"You know how papers are, though. They don't always get the story right. You know anything about it?"

"I was off that day, so I didn't go, but I heard the kid fell from the third floor of a building. Some lady was walking her dog down the alley where it happened and saw the body. She's the one that called us."

"That right? She see anything else?"

"It wasn't my case, so I didn't read it all. But from what I know, the lady called us as soon as she saw the body. I don't remember hearing that she saw anybody or anything else."

"So it was ruled an accident?"

"I'd guess so. I don't think anyone was arrested."

All of a sudden, Barclay stopped and took a long

look at Williams. "Joel, you know something about this case? Is there something I should know?"

"No. I mean, I don't have any facts that you don't have. But I keep wondering how a boy who was supposed to be in a secured school managed to get to a construction site when he was marked as attending all his classes that day."

"I honestly don't know all that much about the case. Like I said, it wasn't one of mine. But maybe I could read up on it a little."

"I'd really appreciate it."

Barclay took a quick glance at his watch. "Look, I got to go. You want me to call you?"

"If you could."

"All right, then."

Williams pulled a leather card case out of his pocket, withdrew a card, and laid it on the table. Then, he wrote a telephone number on the back of the card and, pointing to it, said, "That's my cell number if you need it." He pushed the card across the table to Barclay, who nodded and put the card in his pocket.

Williams and Barclay finished the last of their meal, stood up and put their jackets on. The mist had gotten more persistent, but the trip back to headquarters wasn't long. When they got there, Barclay said, "I better get back in there."

"OK, I'll talk to you soon. Good seeing you."

"You, too, Joel."

The two men shook hands and Williams crossed the street to where his car was parked while Barclay went inside.

Jered Carr was just finishing a meeting of the Committee on Faculty Policies where they'd been talking about changes to Delaware River University's existing tenure system. The meeting had been contentious, as he'd expected it would be. People tended to have very strong feelings about the tenure process. He was a little discouraged, too, as the group hadn't really made any progress at all, and they were expected to send a draft of the committee's recommendations to the full Faculty Senate in two weeks. Carr was hoping that the committee would revamp the process at least a little. He'd be up for tenure the year after next, and he personally thought that the system was too cumbersome right now – too many committees had too much say over who did and didn't get tenure.

That was all right, though. As soon as this meeting was over, he'd be on his way to the WDRU, the university's radio station. Jered loved music, especially blues and early classic rock, and served as a DJ at the radio station. It worked out very well for him; he was able to indulge his passion while at the same time meeting his obligation to serve the university. His thoughts were jerked back from his upcoming playlist when the committee chair finally adjourned the meeting.

As the committee members gathered their papers and folders and scraped their chairs back from the conference room table where they'd been working, Carr's telephone vibrated. Mentally patting himself on the back for remembering to put the phone on "vibrate" before the meeting, Carr pulled it out of his pocket and saw that the caller was Joel Williams.

"Hey, Joel," Carr said as he left the conference room.

"How are you, Jered? Did I catch you at a bad time?"

"Oh, no – just leaving a meeting and heading over for my DJ shift."

"Do you want me to call you back?"

"No, go ahead. What's up?"

"I wanted to catch up with you and Ben about our paper. I think it'd be good for us to have a meeting and see where we are."

"I agree. Do you want to do a Skype meeting?"

"I'd like that. We can share files that way. Can you do a meeting tomorrow morning? I know it's Saturday, but I would like to talk about this stuff."

"Yeah, that's fine, depending on what time you want to meet."

"How about nine-thirty?"

"Got it."

"Good. I'll check with Ben and see if he's free and then get back to you, OK?"

"OK, talk to you later."

Jered finished the call and put his telephone back in his pocket. He was looking forward to comparing notes with Ben and Joel. Maybe between them they'd get answers to the questions they had about Curtis Templeton. The more he thought about it, the surer he was that something was being covered up. Carr wasn't usually the conspiracy-theorist kind, but he'd gotten very little useful information from the school, and Curtis' mother hadn't been any more helpful. Well, maybe Joel had gotten some good information from the students he talked to. And Ben had said he was going to Second Chance today; he might have gotten something useful.

Chapter Six

At nine-twenty the next morning, Jered Carr poured his second cup of tea and carried it into the small home office off the living room. He put the cup down slowly on the edge of the built-in desk, pulled out the large, comfortable black leather chair he'd gotten himself as a treat, and sat down. He turned on his computer and when it had booted up, activated his Skype program. Moments later, he was connected with Joel and Ben. After everyone had greeted each other, Williams started the meeting.

"Thanks for being willing to get together on a Saturday."

"Not a problem," Ben said.

"Not for me, either," Jered said.

"All right, let's take a look at some of our data and see what we've got."

"OK," Ben said. "I'm sending each of you a spreadsheet of the attendance and grade information I've gotten from the Cobbs Creek Center, Second Chance headquarters and the City. I'm a little concerned, because I found an odd discrepancy. If you'll notice, the attendance data that I got from

Cobbs Creek and the data I got from the City match. But neither of them matches what Lauren gave us from headquarters. And I went over this stuff a few times. Take a look and see what you two think."

There was a pause as Jered and Joel received and opened the spreadsheet that Ben had sent them. After a few moments, Jered said, "I see what you mean, Ben. Do you think maybe some of the numbers you got are wrong?"

"That's one possibility. But then the question is, which data is wrong and why is there a discrepancy?"

"Could you get hold of the original records? Maybe see where all of this came from?" Joel asked.

"That's what I'm going to try to do on Monday. I'm going to contact Sheldon Adler and see if he can give me that information. Then maybe we can see what's going on with those numbers."

After a few moments of silence, Jered decided to bring up the topic all of them had in the backs of their minds. "What do we know about Curtis Templeton?"

"One of the students I spoke to said that on the day before he died, Curtis had something on his mind – something that he didn't understand," Joel said.

"Did he say what?"

"No, that's just the thing. He didn't"

"And nothing strange happened at the school that day?"

"Not from what I heard," Joel responded. "But I decided to ask a couple of questions. I had lunch with a cop friend of mine who works at the 19th District in West Philadelphia. They were the ones who investigated Curtis Templeton's death. He's going to see what he can find out and get back to me."

"Good," Jered said. "I had an odd interview with Curtis' mother."

"What do you mean, 'odd?'" Ben asked.

"Well, you'd think parents whose child was killed while under school supervision would jump at the chance to sue the school. At least they'd want to blame the school. But that's not what I heard from this mother – her name is Shanita Finley. She didn't blame the school at all."

"That is unusual," Joel said. "It doesn't tell us a lot, though."

"No," agreed Jered. "But all of this is making me think maybe Curtis' death isn't what it seems. I'm just starting to get the feeling something's going on at that school."

"Well, I'll hopefully be able to check up on that attendance information on Monday," Ben said, "And, Joel, if you hear from your friend, that could help us, too. Then we'll know where we are."

"Well, there isn't anything else we can do right now with the Curtis Templeton question. Let's start talking about what we'll put together for Tuesday." Ben said.

"Are we scheduled to give a presentation?" asked Joel.

"Not as far as I know. I just want us to have some preliminary findings to share in case we get asked."

"Good idea," Jered said.

For the next few minutes, the three men reviewed the basic findings they'd put together. Except for this one death, the program really did seem to be successful. All three men felt comfortable saying

[133]

that, overall, Second Chance students were more likely to stay out of trouble and get an education than young people in other programs. And Second Chance students were even more likely to do well than those in the juvenile justice system. Once they'd agreed on the conclusions that they could share, Jered said, "What are we going to say about Curtis Templeton? On Tuesday, I mean."

"We don't have enough information to say anything, really," Joel replied. "We'll say that our conclusions are preliminary and that we're still working on our data. And that's the truth."

"I guess so," said Ben. "It is true, and it gives me time to figure out what's going on with that attendance data. But I think there's something to Curtis' death."

"To be perfectly honest, I'm getting there, myself," said Joel, thinking of what Marisol had told him. "But we don't have any real facts. Certainly no evidence. And we can't make wild accusations. Besides, we're not police. It's their job to investigate crime."

"I agree," Ben said. "I'm not saying we should say anything at the dinner, especially with no proof. But

I wouldn't be surprised if it turns out that there's something funny going on."

"Let's wait until we know more," Joel said. "Ben, you'll be getting that data straightened out, we hope. That will give us more of what we need for our study. And as for Curtis Templeton, if I hear anything, I'll let you know. For now, I think we have what we need for that dinner."

"All right," Jered said, a little unwillingly. "I guess I'll see you all on Tuesday, then. Lauren says that the bar opens at six o'clock, and dinner is at seven. How about if we meet there a little early – maybe five-thirty – so that we have time to talk if we need to?"

"All right," Joel said.

"That works for me," Ben said.

The three men agreed to meet in the hotel ballroom and in the meantime, to keep in touch by telephone and email as they needed to. Soon afterwards, they ended the Skype meeting.

Jered was pulling out his chair from his desk when he heard the sound of Lauren's car pulling into their driveway. She'd been out buying groceries while he was meeting with Ben and Joel, and her car would probably be loaded with bags. He straightened up and went through the kitchen door into the garage, where he stopped to put on the sneakers he kept there. Then, he walked out to Lauren's car.

"Want some help unloading?"

"Thanks," she smiled.

For the next few minutes, neither spoke as they carried the bags of food into the kitchen.

When all of the bags were inside, Lauren asked, "So how did your meeting go?"

"Pretty well, thanks. We're going to meet early on Tuesday, so we can talk before everything gets started."

"That's a good idea."

"We're hoping to meet up at the Riverton at five-thirty. I hope you don't mind getting there that early."

"No, that's fine. You guys aren't scheduled to give a presentation, are you?"

"Not as far as I know. We just want to have one ready if people have questions for us."

"That makes sense."

[136]

"The only problem," Jered said, "might be that Ben found something strange in the attendance data he got."

"You mean the stuff I gave you?"

"Well, partly. The attendance information Ben got from Cobbs Creek matches what he got from the City of Philadelphia."

"Yeah, the City uses that data to authorize payment to Second Chance per the contract we have with them."

"Right. But the thing is, that data doesn't match what you gave us."

"I'm not sure what you mean."

"After the groceries are put away, I'll show you."

Lauren agreed and for the next few minutes, the two of them emptied the bags. Then, Jered said, "OK, let's go."

Lauren followed her husband to their office where the spreadsheets Ben had sent were still open on the computer. "Here," said Jered, "This is what I mean."

Jered pointed to the screen to show Lauren the differences in the data sets.

[137]

"Do you see how the attendance data from Cobbs Creek and the City show more students than the data you gave me?"

"I do see it, but it doesn't make sense. I pulled that information from the same figures that Cobbs Creek sent to the City. It should have been identical."

"You mean the attendance numbers get sent directly from Cobbs Creek to your office?"

"Yeah. The students' names and information are stored at Cobbs Creek, and they send us email copies of the information. Then the information gets stored in our Cobbs Creek database. That's where I got it. There's no reason that information should be different."

"Well, do you think you could maybe trace that data? Find out who sent it?"

Lauren rubbed her forehead in an effort to think "Jered, I don't know. I can't just go poking around the data without people asking questions. Do you really think something's wrong?"

"Please?"

Lauren bit her lower lip. At last, she reluctantly agreed. "OK. But I'm not promising anything."

"I know. And I appreciate it."

That night, Ben Peterson sat on his living room sofa
staring at the same printouts. He kept thinking that
if he could figure out exactly what the differences
were between the two sets of numbers, he might get
to the bottom of whatever was going on. He finally
got a pencil out and began drawing lines through
students' names that were in all of the data sets. In
the end, he was left with fifteen names. There were
fifteen students whose names were on the lists he'd
gotten from the Cobbs Creek attendance records
and the City records, but weren't on the records
from Second Chance headquarters.

Ben wrote down the fifteen names on a separate list.
They could be students at another Second Chance
center whose names had mistakenly gotten placed
on the Cobbs Creek list. But that didn't make sense.
Wouldn't the Cobbs Creek staff know who was
enrolled at that center? Maybe they were students
who had originally been sent to Cobbs Creek but,
for whatever reason, withdrew after their names had
been listed in the attendance data. Or, they could be

students who were sent to the Cobbs Creek center after the attendance information had been sent to headquarters, but before it was sent to the City. That made more sense, especially since the dates on the Cobbs Creek and City of Philadelphia information were more recent than the date on the information that had been sent to headquarters. Still, he couldn't be sure. He'd talk to Sheldon Adler and Therese Vaughan about it on Monday.

For his part, Joel Williams spent the weekend doing battle with the autumn leaves in his yard. He often found that doing yard work and other chores helped him think, and he wanted very much to think. He wasn't particularly worried about the research team's study. Ben knew what he was doing when it came to analyzing data. He'd find anything there was to find. And Jered was a dependable research partner, too; he'd gotten some solid information and he'd be very helpful when it came to getting the paper ready to present at conferences. But something about what was going on at Second Chance bothered him. It was partly Curtis Templeton's death. Actually, a lot of it was that.

But it was more. It was Curtis' mother's reaction. It was what Marisol had said. It was that attendance data, too. Something just didn't feel right.

That Sunday evening, Williams went on an after-dinner trip to the gym. He had grading to do and wanted to be alert for it. When he got back, he took a quick shower and settled in the living room to read some student assignments. He was on the third one when he was interrupted by his telephone's trill.

"Hello?"

"Joel? It's Shirley Mizzello. Do you have a minute?"

"Of course. What's on your mind?"

"It's that new center that the dean announced."

Williams was afraid that was why she was calling. This could take some time. With a barely-controlled sigh, he sat down again on the sofa.

"I know you had some concerns about it."

"You're damned right I do. You know I try not to let things get to me, but I think we're headed for real problems with this center."

"You do?"

"Yes, and I'm not the only one. A few of us are really concerned about this, and we want to meet with the dean. I'd love it if you'd come with us."

"I'm honestly not sure what I can add, Shirley. You know the faculty policies in and out."

"But aren't you doing a study of one of those for-profit options?"

"That's true, I am," Williams said. "But it's an alternative school, not really a prison alternative."

"Same difference. Your findings might be able to help us."

Williams hesitated a minute. Another commitment was the last thing he needed right now. Still, Shirley was a departmental colleague. "All right," he finally said. "When's the meeting with the dean?"

"We're going to try to set it up tomorrow, and I'll get back to you with the day and time."

"OK"

"Thanks, Joel," she said as they ended the conversation.

Williams tried to return to his papers. He wanted to give them back to his students the next day, and they weren't nearly ready. For a while he concentrated on grading, but his mind kept drifting. He understood exactly what Shirley meant about faculty rights. On the other hand, he and Jared and Ben had found promising results for Second Chance. Why not have a university research center for alternatives like it? Second Chance seemed to be doing good things. Except for Curtis Templeton's death.

Curtis Templeton's death. That was another thing. How did he get out of the school unnoticed? And if someone killed him, why? The young people he'd spoken to had hinted that Curtis had a way of finding things out. But that didn't help much, at least not now. Williams glanced over at the pile of student papers silently accusing him. He wasn't any closer to figuring out what happened to Curtis, and he wasn't anywhere close to being finished with his grading. With an exasperated sigh, he turned back to his papers.

On Monday morning, Ben Peterson got to his office earlier than usual. He wanted to get in touch with both Therese Vaughan and Sheldon Adler as soon as he could so that he could get everything organized for the next night. As soon as he'd hung up his lightweight jacket, he sat down at his desk, scrolled through his list of contacts, and located Therese Vaughan's telephone number. Within moments he'd gotten through to her.

"Good morning, Therese. It's Ben Peterson. We met the other day about Second Chance."

"Oh yes, of course. What can I do for you?"

"Well, I've been going over the attendance data you gave me. It's very helpful. But I noticed something odd about it. There are fifteen names on the attendance list you gave me that aren't there on the list I got from Second Chance headquarters."

"Now, that *is* odd. Are you sure?"

"I went over it all a couple of times. I'm pretty sure of what I found."

And you say they're missing from the list you got from Cobbs Creek?"

"No. That's what's strange. What I got from Cobbs Creek matches what I got from you. It's the list I got from headquarters that's different."

"Well, we get our information directly from Cobbs Creek. If you noticed something different about the data, you might want to talk to Sheldon Adler over at Cobbs Creek. He'd be the one to know how they put their attendance information together. If there's a difference between what they sent us and what they sent headquarters, he'll be able to tell you why."

"I'll do that, then. And thanks."

Sheldon Adler had just poured himself a cup of coffee and turned his office computer on when his telephone buzzed. He pulled it out of his pocket.

"Hey, how are you?"

"Look, I don't have time to talk. You were right the other day. We have a problem."

"What do you mean?" asked Adler. "I thought things were under control."

"Well, they're not. I just got off the phone with Ben Peterson. He's been asking about attendance."

"Yeah, he was here the other day, too. He was asking for our attendance records, and I gave him what I sent you."

"Yeah, well, he got records from your headquarters, too, and you know they don't match."

[145]

"I know. He asked about that and I told him it was probably some sort of glitch – you know, names being dropped by accident."

"Did he believe you?"

Adler rubbed the back of his neck and began to pace his office as he spoke. "I think so. Look, don't worry about it. I've got it under control."

"Good. Now, I got to go. Just let me know what happens, OK?"

"I will."

Adler finished his call and sat down at his desk. He picked up a pencil and absently began tapping it on the desktop. Just then, his office phone rang, nearly making him jump.

"Yes?"

"Mr. Adler, it's Ben Peterson."

"Thanks, Patrice. Put him through, please."

"OK."

Adler swallowed hard and put a plastic smile on his face as he said, "Hello, Ben, how are you?"

"Just fine, thanks. How are you?"

"I'm good. What can I do for you?"

"Well, I was looking over the attendance information you gave me. Remember I said it didn't match what I got at headquarters?"

"Yeah, and I mentioned at the time that sometimes names get omitted by accident."

"I'm wondering if I can stop up today and get whatever information you might have on those missing students. I found fifteen names. Do you think you could help me fill in the blanks on those students?"

"OK, I've got meetings this morning. Maybe about two?"

"Two it is. And thanks."

Sheldon Adler hung the phone up. He only had a few hours to figure out what he was going to do.

Lauren Carr glanced around her, took a breath, and went into Grace Wong's office. As Mark Donnelly's Executive Assistant, Grace got most of the paperwork from the three Second Chance centers, so if anyone would know about the attendance data, she would. Grace looked up when Lauren came in.

"Hi, Lauren, how are you?"

[147]

"I'm good, thanks. You?"

"Good, thanks." Grace raised her eyebrows expectantly.

"Sorry to bug you, but I wanted to ask you about those attendance records you gave me the other day."

"Oh, sure. Did they not print out right?"

"Oh, no. They printed out fine. It's just that my husband and his research team are doing a study of Second Chance, and they want to get some details about where the data came from. Do you by chance know who sent the attendance information over?"

"I'd have to look to be sure, but the data from Mayfair is usually sent by Helen Stuart. We get Point Breeze's from AnneMarie Russo, and Cobbs Creek's stuff usually comes from Martine Robertson. Do you need their numbers?"

"That'd be really helpful."

Grace jotted the names and numbers down and gave them to Lauren, who thanked her. Then, hoping to avoid too many questions about what she was doing, Lauren left Grace's office. She still wasn't at all comfortable doing what she thought of as snooping. Still, she was curious about those names that should have been on the attendance list sent to headquarters. Besides, she'd told Jered she would find out what she could. Maybe he or Ben or Joel Williams would be able to use this contact information. When she got back to her office, Lauren put the names and telephone numbers into her purse.

Just before two o'clock, Ben Peterson went into the main office at Second Chance of Cobbs Creek. He gave his name to the student receptionist and waited for Sheldon Adler. When Adler arrived, he shepherded his guest down to his office, offered him a chair and said, "So, you wanted to show me some of that attendance data?"

"Yes. I found fifteen names that were on the overall attendance list that I got from you and from the City, but that weren't on the list I got from headquarters."

"Right. You mentioned that."

"Well, I was wondering if I could show you the names. Maybe you might recognize them or be able to tell me about them."

"Sure, OK."

Peterson pulled the list of names out of the tote he'd brought with him and handed them to Adler, who slowly looked them over. After a few moments, Adler said, "I recognize these names. They're all former students. And you're saying they weren't on the list that you got from headquarters?"

"Right."

"It's hard to say exactly what happened, but like I told you, it was probably just some sort of oversight."

"So, this data – with those names added – is accurate?"

"Yeah, that's the data you should use."

"And that's the data that gets sent to the City?"

"Exactly. And the same data is supposed to get sent to headquarters, too."

"I think I get it. And those attendance records come from each center's attendance information?"

"Right."

"So somehow, the information you folks had here on those fifteen students never made it to headquarters."

"That's what it looks like."

"Any idea how it happened?"

"Could have been lots of things. If the spreadsheet program dropped some names, that'd do it. Or if names didn't get entered into the lists for headquarters, that'd do it, too. But I wouldn't know about that. Martine Robertson, our secretary, sends those lists in."

"Could I ask her about these names?"

"Sure, let's see if she's at her desk."

The two men left Adler's office and returned to the main office where Adler introduced Peterson to Martine Robertson, a lively brunette with long puce fingernails. After the introductions, Ben handed the list of names to Martine. "Does this list of names look familiar?"

Martine looked at the names, then said, "Seems to me I do remember some of these names, anyway. Let me look and see."

Her nails clacked on the keyboard as she looked for the files she wanted.

"Yeah, here it is. See, this is the attendance sheet we prepared for you. And this is the report I sent to the City. We send one every year."

"The funny thing is, though, that these names aren't on the list that I got from headquarters."

"What? That's weird. They should be. Lemme see that."

Peterson handed her a copy of the data from headquarters.

Martine shook her head. "I have no idea how that happened. The only thing I can think of is that maybe some names got chopped off the files by accident up at headquarters. Or maybe somebody up there forgot some names or something."

Ben could see how a software glitch or a human error might explain the loss of one or two names. But fifteen seemed a bit much. Still, he didn't want to accuse anyone of lying if he didn't have proof. And if Adler, Robertson, or both, were lying, they weren't about to admit it. He decided to let the matter drop for the moment, at least until he had something more concrete. "Yeah, you're probably right," he said. He took the papers back, thanked both Martine Robertson and her boss for their time, and left.

That evening, the three researchers held another Skype conference. Not really satisfied with the answers he'd gotten from Cobbs Creek, Ben had called both Joel and Jered and asked if they could talk about what they'd learned. Both men had agreed. Now, all three men were looking at the list of names that Ben had sent the other two.

"What I haven't figured out," Ben said, "is why those names would be left off of the list we got from Second Chance headquarters. I'm beginning to think it was deliberate, because it just doesn't make sense that so many names would accidentally be missed. Not the way this software is laid out."

"Let's backtrack a minute," Joel said. "All of the names on the attendance data we got are names of Cobbs Creek students, right?"

"Right," Ben replied.

"Cobbs Creek's attendance data goes to the City, and the City then pays Second Chance based on enrollment, right?"

"Yeah," Ben said slowly. He was beginning to see where Joel was going with this. So was Jered.

"So what you're suggesting," Jered said, "is that those fifteen names weren't left off of the headquarters list deliberately..."

"Exactly," Joel responded, "They might have been added to Cobbs Creek deliberately."

There was silence as the three men thought about what this meant. Then, Ben said, "And somebody doesn't want headquarters to know about this."

"Right," Jered said slowly. Then, he said, "What about our study? It would take a lot of legwork to prove this, although what you're saying makes sense, Joel. If we back out now, we'd have to explain ourselves, and that could be really awkward."

"But if we go ahead and publish this stuff, we could be using fraudulent data," Ben replied.

"For right now," Joel said, "let's just catch our breaths. We'll be seeing Mark Donnelly and some of the other Second Chance administrators tomorrow night. While we're there, let's ask them for a meeting, so we can all sit down and talk about this."

"I guess that makes sense," Ben said.

"Agreed," Jered said.

"OK, I don't think there's anything else we can do tonight. We'll get this all settled soon."

Chapter Seven

The next morning dawned cold and crisp, with a clear, sunny sky. It was a beautiful autumn morning, and Mark Donnelly thought it boded well for Information Night that night. The changeable weather was always a factor at this time of year. But it seemed they were in luck; there wasn't a cloud in sight. Donnelly smiled to himself as he looked out of his living room window at the riot of reds, golds, oranges, and browns on the trees outside. If he and his team did their jobs that night, they'd impress the people from the City of Wilmington that he'd invited. That could mean a contract with Wilmington. They might also get contracts from Philadelphia for new centers. Things were looking good.

Lauren Carr looked at her reflection in the bathroom mirror as she combed her wavy auburn hair. She was going to have to do an extra-careful job on her makeup this morning to cover up her lack of sleep; those dark circles would be sure to show up against her clear Celtic complexion. She hadn't been able to rest easily after Jered told her about his Skype meeting with Ben Peterson and Joel Williams. Lauren had only met Williams a few times, but he seemed like a fairly sensible and intuitive guy. And Williams was saying that somebody could be padding Second Chance's attendance lists. It upset Lauren to think that someone, maybe someone at the company, was stealing money. The question was, should she do anything about it? Since the padded list hadn't been sent to headquarters, whoever was stealing money probably wasn't someone she worked with directly. But shouldn't she report it anyway? On the other hand, Lauren hadn't bargained for this. She could be asking for a lot of trouble if she stirred anything up. Her thoughts whirled as she leaned closer to the mirror, trying to cover up her exhaustion with foundation as best she could.

"You OK?" Jered asked.

Lauren started, then recovered herself as she turned around. "Yeah, I guess. This whole thing has me upset."

"I know it does."

"Jered, I didn't sign up to be a whistleblower."

"Look, maybe this thing has some sort of rational explanation. We're going to be talking to Mark Donnelly and some other people at the dinner and presentation tonight. He may be able to answer our questions."

"Maybe," Lauren shook her head, "but I'm not so sure."

"I'm not, either. And I'm sorry you have to deal with this."

"It's not your fault, Jered. I just hope we get some answers."

"I do, too." Jered squeezed his wife's shoulder and she smiled into the mirror at his reflection. Then he turned to go downstairs and put together the playlist he wanted for that day's radio show.

At nine-thirty, Ben Peterson returned to his office after his Tuesday morning class. He typically didn't like teaching at eight o'clock in the morning, but this morning, he was glad. He wanted to get back to the Second Chance data. When he got into his office, he checked his phone for messages. Finding none, he opened up the data set on his computer. After one more look through it to make sure he hadn't missed anything, Ben called Therese Vaughan.

"I've got a couple of questions," Ben said once they were connected. "I'm hoping you can help me."

"Well, I'll try. But if it's about that Second Chance information, all I can tell you is what I said yesterday. We get our attendance information directly from Second Chance. I have no way of knowing what goes on at their offices."

"I know. What I wanted to ask you about is something a bit different. You manage the City's contract with Second Chance, right?"

"That's right. I keep the files and paperwork, visit the school sites periodically, and sign off on the funding."

"That's what I thought. What I really wanted to ask you about is that process."

"The funding?"

"Right. I just want to understand how that works, so that I can write it up accurately in the paper we're doing. From what I understand, if a program like

Second Chance wants to be funded, it first has to be approved by the District, right?"

"Yes, we don't fund programs that aren't District-approved."

"And then the program applies for funding. Is that what happens next?"

"Right. The program that's applying for funding has to file the initial paperwork, and then we do a visit and make a determination. If the decision is favorable, we start funding the program."

"And your funding per year is based on the number of students in the program. Is that right?"

"That's right."

"Got it. Thanks." Ben had the information he'd been looking for. Joel had been right. This was probably all about getting more funding from the City of Philadelphia. He wondered if Therese Vaughan knew about what Second Chance might be doing. If she did know, she was probably involved. He didn't have any authority to confront her directly and he knew that if she was involved, she'd probably lie, anyway. So, Ben made a note to himself and ended their conversation as quickly as he could. He'd talk to Joel and Jered about what options the team might have for alerting the authorities.

Joel Williams opened up his email for a quick check. He was planning to be away from the office for most of the day and wanted to make sure he didn't miss anything important. The only red-flagged note he got was from Ed Beaumont, Chair of the Department of Criminal Justice:

Hi, Everyone,
I know it's not our usual week for a meeting, but we need to get together next week to talk about the new center. Let me know if you're free Wednesday morning, and we'll go from there.
Thanks,
EB

Williams shook his head a little. He liked working with Ed – he felt lucky about that. But emails were not one of Ed's strengths. People who didn't know him well often thought that Ed was brusque for that reason. Well, whatever Ed had in mind was going to have to wait for a bit. Williams had decided to take a side trip this morning to get a look at Second Chance's Cobbs Creek Center before heading out to Valley Forge. It meant an extra few hours in the car, but it would also give him time to himself. This new center could upset a lot of people. More than that, it had implications for the school and department. It was time to start thinking about where he stood on the issues. It didn't help that there wasn't a lot of information yet, but he'd have to do the best he could with what there was. After a quick response to Ed, confirming he'd be there on Wednesday, Williams shut down his computer and get ready to leave Tilton.

Two hours later, and not much closer to a decision about the new center, Williams parked his Dodge a block away from Second Chance of Cobbs Creek. He got out of his car and, after locking it, walked towards the building. As he approached it, Williams saw two people just leaving. One he recognized as Mark Donnelly from Second Chance headquarters. The other was a heavyset, middle-aged woman. The two stood in the doorway for a moment. Then they left, heading for separate cars.

Williams went up the steps to the building and, after going through the metal detector, looked around the empty foyer. There'd been a security guard on duty when he'd been there the first time, but he didn't see one now. Just then, a small door off to the left opened and the guard came out. He approached Williams and asked, "Can I help you?"

"Yes, thanks." Williams thought quickly. "I'm Joel Williams, part of a research team that's doing a study of Second Chance. I thought I just saw Mark Donnelly from headquarters leave the building. Do you know if he's coming back?"

"Sorry," the security guard said. "I didn't hear him say anything about whether he's coming back later. You want to leave a message? They can take a message in the office."

"Um, no, thanks. I think I'll just give him a call later up at headquarters. It's not urgent."

"OK, then," said the guard.

Williams thanked him and left, so as not to encourage any questions. He walked back out into

[163]

the bright sunlight, squinting a bit as he returned to his car. When he reached it, he got in and sat for a few minutes, staring out the window. That security guard hadn't been in the foyer when Williams arrived; he'd been in the restroom. Even a quick trip to the restroom was long enough for an alert kid. And it looked as though people did enter and leave the building during the day. If Curtis Templeton picked his time well, it'd be possible for him to simply slip out behind someone who was leaving, especially if that someone was either talking to somebody else or carrying a package or otherwise distracted. It could happen. Williams thought about the logistics of it as he slowly pulled out of his parking spot and began the trip north and west to Valley Forge, where the Riverton Hotel was located.

Lauren Carr stood at the open door to Mark Donnelly's office. That morning, he'd asked her to stop in after lunch, probably to go over what they would tell potential investors at Information Night, though he hadn't been specific. She was normally excited about attracting new investors. She'd taken the job at Second Chance because she'd believed the program was a good one, and Jered and his team had found some promising results. But the more she thought about what had happened to Curtis Templeton, the more questions she had about what might really be going on at the Cobbs Creek Center. And now this whole business about padding the attendance lists with nonexistent students. She wasn't sure what to believe any more about Second Chance.

"Oh, hi, Lauren, have a seat," Mark said when he saw her at the door. "Thanks for coming in."

"Sure, no problem," Lauren answered.

"I just wanted to check with you about tonight. You and Jered will be there, right?"

"We sure will."

"Good. The people from the City of Wilmington will be there, and some of the City people from Philadelphia. I want us to make as good an impression as we can."

"I know. This is an important night."

"And that's what I wanted to talk to you about. Do you know what Jered and his team have prepared for this evening?"

Lauren paused for only a second. "No, not really. I know they've found some good results, but they haven't given me details."

"It's just that they're going to want to make a good impression, too. There'll be people there who could be of help to them, so they'll want to make sure to have all their ducks in a row."

"Oh, I think they'll be ready."

"I'm glad. It's going to be important that they focus on what they can really support."

"Mark, what are you getting at?"

"You got me," Donnelly said, holding up his hands in mock surrender. "I want to know if they're planning to talk about Curtis Templeton."

"I don't know exactly what they've prepared. What makes you think they're going to bring up Curtis Templeton?' Lauren asked carefully.

"Well, I had dinner with Ben Peterson the other night, and he was asking about the whole thing. Then, Sheldon Adler down at Cobbs Creek told me Peterson had been talking to him about it, too."

"I guess it's natural they'd ask about him. That was a tragedy."

"It was, and that's what I told Ben. But it was a tragic accident. It was a one-time event – not something you want to build a study around. Not if you want credibility. I'm just saying I hope they keep in mind that their reputation is on the line here."

"I know they're taking it seriously, Mark."

"Good, that's all I wanted to know. You may want to say something to Jered too, so we we're sure we're all on the same page."

"Of course," Lauren answered. This was definitely one of the strangest conversations she'd ever had with Mark, and it worried her. He was essentially telling her to warn the research team against saying anything about a Second Chance student's death. Lauren wasn't an academic, but she certainly knew that if a research study was going to be accurate, it couldn't gloss over things. And even though Mark was right that one incident wasn't enough to make assumptions, Curtis' death was an important event. It should be in the study. And then there were those differences between the attendance records at Cobbs

Creek and the City, and the records at headquarters. The more Lauren thought about it, the more convinced she was that somebody at Second Chance was covering up some serious things.

"Was there anything you wanted to talk about?" Mark asked. Lauren realized she must have been standing there silently longer than she'd thought.

"Oh, no, thanks. I think we're on track for tonight. I'd better get back to my office."

"OK, I'll see you later then."

"OK."

Sitting in his home office, Jered Carr took another look at the notes he'd made of his conversation with Shanita Finley. He wondered again whether there was some sort of agreement between her and Second Chance. He couldn't think of any other logical reason she'd be so reticent and so unwilling to blame the school or the teachers. Even if he was wrong about that, Carr wanted to bring the topic up when he saw Joel Williams and Ben Peterson that evening. He tucked the notes into his open briefcase, snapped it shut and straightened up. He took the briefcase into the foyer and set it on the floor by the front door, so he wouldn't forget it. Then he went upstairs to change his clothes before he left to meet Lauren, Ben and Joel at the Riverton.

The traffic out of Philadelphia towards Valley Forge was getting heavier as Ben Peterson drove to the Riverton. Still, the weather had stayed clear, so at least there wouldn't be any rain or early snow to slow things down even more. As he drove, Peterson's mind was rapidly ticking off the points he was hoping the research team would make that night. Their approach had been solid – that, he knew. And he was confident that the numbers he'd gotten and the results he'd found could be trusted. Had he remembered the PowerPoint files? Yes, they were loaded on his laptop and ready to go. He'd printed out his notes, too, and those were ready. He was sure that Joel and Jered would be ready, too. The only question was what to do with the information they'd found about the attendance records. There was the matter of Curtis Templeton, too. Fortunately, the research team would be meeting with Mark Donnelly and some of the other Second Chance staff before dinner. Hopefully,

Williams had been right, and they'd be able to straighten everything out. Peterson wasn't one to leave things until the last minute, and it bothered him not to have everything completely ready. But as he saw it, he really didn't have a choice. He resigned himself to not being as thoroughly prepared as he'd have liked and focused on the drive.

The late-afternoon sun slanted through the trees alongside the highway as Peterson got to Valley Forge. Ten minutes and a wrong turn later, he'd arrived at the Riverton. Second Chance had chosen the hotel carefully. It was a large, well-restored building, built in the late Colonial style, with a graceful curved driveway and a large parking lot discreetly off to the left. Peterson soon found a spot and went into the hotel. He glanced around the lobby to see if any others had arrived. The lobby was nearly empty, but an elegantly-lettered sign directed him down a hall to his right towards the main ballroom. He'd go there soon, but first he wanted to check in. He'd decided to take a room for the night to spare himself the long drive back to Delaware.

When Peterson had gotten to his room and dropped his things off, he took the elevator from his fourth-floor room to the ballroom. He saw that Joel Williams was already there and went over to greet him.

"Hey, you made it," he said.

"Yeah, I was in Philadelphia today anyway, so I decided to try to beat the traffic."

"Smart move. It can be pretty bad."

"You all ready?"

"Oh, yeah, I'm just concerned about what we're going to do about the attendance stuff and about Curtis Templeton."

"It's going to depend a lot on what we hear from Mark Donnelly and his staff."

"I know. I just hope they get here before everything gets started."

The two men looked up as Jered and Lauren Carr came in.

"Glad you're here," Joel said as they approached.

[171]

"Thanks," Jered said as they shook hands. Lauren
smiled mechanically.

"Why don't we find a place to sit down and put our
heads together for a few minutes," Ben said.

The four of them chose a table in one of the corners
and sat down. "OK," Joel said, "Let's do a final
run-through of what we're going to say."

For the next few minutes, the research team
discussed their plan for their presentation. It was a
while before anyone noticed that Lauren hadn't said
anything.

Jered recognized the signs that something was
troubling his wife.

"What do you think, hon?" he asked. "Are we
ready?"

"I think so," she said absently.

"Something wrong?" he asked.

Lauren thought for a second. "Actually, there is
something I need to tell you guys. It's something
Mark Donnellly told me this afternoon."

When Lauren saw that she had the three men's
attention, she went on. "He basically told me to tell
you not to mention Curtis Templeton at all. That it

wouldn't do your reputations any good to focus on just one incident. He said you have the chance to make a good impression tonight and he'd hate to see you blow it."

After a moment, Ben said, "And I found out how the funding process works between the City and the schools. It could very easily be a case of padding attendance rolls and skimming off the extra money, just like you thought, Joel."

Everyone sat quietly, digesting all of this. Somehow, it all fit together; it was just a matter of figuring out how. Just then, Ben looked up, his face alert. "I just thought of something. What if Curtis Templeton –"

At that moment, the ballroom doors swung open and Mark Donnelly came in. With him were Sheldon Adler and a few other members of the Second Chance staff. When Donnelly saw the group seated at the table, he called out, "Hey, you made it! That's great! Are we good to go?"

The three researchers and Lauren Carr looked at each other for a moment. Then Williams said, "I think we're good to go for tonight. But we've got some concerns about the project that we think we should discuss. Could we set up a meeting with you in the next couple of days?"

"Sure. Anything I can answer for you or clarify right now?"

Ben Peterson said, "Well, I'm still really concerned about the death of Curtis Templeton."

"As are we all," Donnelly replied. "That's why we took that tragic accident very seriously and have taken all the measures I mentioned to you the other night. But I'm sure you folks know better than to base your study on one incident, even a tragic one. I'm sure your remarks are going to be more solidly-grounded than that. But we can certainly talk about Curtis Templeton at our meeting if you still have concerns."

"I think we should," Peterson replied. "It's not just the death, though. I'm also concerned about the attendance data and the difference between what's in the City's and Cobbs Creek's records, and what's in your headquarters' records. I think there's a real problem there, and I'd be glad of any information you can give us."

"I know you've been concerned about that, and I'm glad you've brought it up. Why not get all of your numbers together and we'll sit down and talk about it before the end of the week. I'm sure we can figure out precisely what's going on."

Peterson wasn't taken in by Donnelly's assurances, but he also didn't want to make a scene. People were beginning to come into the ballroom in twos and threes, and he wanted the research team to make a good impression. "All right," he said. "I'll call you tomorrow, OK?"

"Sounds great. Now, if you'll excuse me, I need to mingle. You know how it is."

Donnelly nodded and smiled at the group and took his leave. Adler said, "Mark Donnelly's a good guy. I'm sure he'll help you straighten everything out. I need to go mingle, too, but let me know if you have any questions."

"Thanks," murmured Jered.

Ben said, "I think we need to report exactly what we've found – including the attendance data. And Curtis Templeton."

Joel nodded his head slowly. "I see your point. Let's do it this way. Let's simply state our overall findings, just the way we went over it. Then, we can say at the end that our findings are tentative, and that we don't have complete attendance information yet."

"What about Curtis?" Jered asked.

"I say we mention him, too. We were going to mention the school's safety policies and record, anyway, and we can say that in that one case, those policies failed, and had to be revamped," Ben answered.

Everyone agreed to this, and the group got ready to mix with the other guests who'd been steadily arriving for the past ten minutes. Ben decided to use the restroom first, so he excused himself and crossed the large ballroom back to the main lobby where small signs pointed out the room he was looking for. When he'd finished, he entered the lobby again and as he walked back towards the ballroom, noticed Therese Vaughan and Sheldon Adler having an animated conversation. Adler noticed Peterson too and waved him over to join them.

"It sounded like you folks are all ready to go," Adler said.

"I think so."

"Good," said Vaughan.

Adler said, "And you have everything you need?"

Peterson carefully said, "I still have a lot of questions and concerns, as you heard me tell Mark Donnelly. But I think we have what we need for this evening, thanks."

"Well," Adler said, "I'm sure Mark will be able to help you straighten everything out. For now, I'm glad you've got the data you need. There are some influential people in there, and you'll be able to impress them."

Vaughan nodded, "I know I'm looking forward to what you have to say. I think Second Chance is a good program."

Peterson said, "There's a lot good about it. That's part of what upsets me about the attendance records and about Curtis Templeton's death. Things like that tarnish a program's reputation."

"Exactly," Vaughan said. Adler added, "Which is why I was glad to hear you'll be focusing on the solid aggregate data that you do have instead of mentioning individual students. Your presentation will be a lot stronger that way and, I admit it, it'll make Second Chance look better, too."

Ben looked at both of them. "I'm not sure you understand. We're certainly going to mention some of the larger findings we've had. But our study isn't complete, and we're going to report that, too. We don't have accurate attendance figures, for one thing. And Curtis Templeton's death is important."
"So you're planning to bring that up, too?" Adler asked.
"We're going to have to if we're going to tell the truth."
"But that was one incident – a tragic accident."
"And we're not going to claim that it's anything else. But it's part of our study."
Adler said, "I'm not sure this is the right time to bring that up – not with this crowd. Maybe we can find a way to discuss it in your final report, but tonight? I'm not so sure it's the best idea."

[178]

Ben had already guessed that both Vaughan and Adler knew more than they'd told him. This last comment of Adler's simply made him surer He didn't have time to discuss it any further, though, and besides, he didn't have proof. Not real proof. So, he simply said, "Thanks for your views, Sheldon, I appreciate it." Then he smiled thinly and started back to the ballroom.

All of a sudden, he stopped and cursed quietly to himself. He'd left the handouts he'd prepared in his room. Glancing at his watch, he cursed again and went quickly to the bank of elevators across the lobby. He punched the "Up" button and when the elevator arrived, dashed on board. At the fourth floor, Peterson got off the elevator and practically ran down the hall to his room. He jammed his card into the card slot and opened the door. He pushed it all the way back so that it would stay open, since he was only planning to grab his handouts. He'd just picked the papers up when he heard a noise behind him and looked up in surprise at the figure standing framed in the doorway.

[179]

Thalia Bradley was standing outside one of the side entrances to the Riverton Hotel. She hated the hotel's smoke-free policy and wished she didn't have to go outside every time she wanted a cigarette. She'd just lit up when a noise from above caught her attention. She looked up, her cigarette forgotten, as a man came flying down from what must have been one of the upper floors. As his body hit the side parking lot with a sickening thump, Thalia screamed and ran around the building to the front entrance. Barely controlling herself, she rushed up to the receptionist calling out, "Call 911! Somebody just fell off a balcony!" Outside, a sheaf of papers fluttered down and scattered in the crisp breeze.

Chapter Eight

In the ballroom, Joel Williams was waiting for the bartender to hand him a beer when Jered Carr tapped him on the shoulder.

"I can't find Ben," he said. "He isn't anywhere in the room and we need to get started soon. Have you seen him?"

Williams took a swallow of his beer and shook his head. "No, I haven't. But I think he took a room for the night. He could be up in his room. Maybe he forgot something up there."

Jered's face cleared. "Yeah, that's probably it. I'll go out in the lobby and call him. It's too loud in here."

"All right."

Jered crossed the crowded ballroom and went towards the lobby. When he got there, he saw that chaos had erupted. One woman – probably another guest – was sitting on one of the lobby chairs talking to the hotel manager. Three hotel security guards were standing at the reception desk speaking to one of the receptionists. Another receptionist was

[181]

doing his best to cope with a line of people waiting to check in. Just then, Jered heard the loud wail of a police siren. Two police cars had pulled into the hotel's driveway. Moments later, two officers strode into the lobby. The manager said something to the woman he was talking to and rose to meet the police officers. With a subtle gesture, he indicated the guest sitting on the lobby couch and the officers went over to speak to her. In a moment or two, the three of them rose, left the lobby area and followed the manager to what Jered guessed was the manager's office.

Just then Jered heard another siren. He had no idea what was going on, but it must be serious. He remembered then that he was supposed to be calling Ben and pulled his own phone out of his pocket. He scrolled through his list of numbers until he found Ben's. Then he pushed the "Call" button. After several rings, Jered heard Ben's recording. Damn! He pushed the "Call" button again. Again, Ben didn't answer. Now Jered was getting concerned. He was getting ready to go to the reception desk and ask for Ben's room number when his phone rang.

Glancing down at the screen, he saw that it was Ben's number.

"Ben, where are you?" Jered asked. "We're waiting for you, so we can get started."

A strange male voice said, "Sir, this is the Phoenixville Police. Can you identify yourself, please?"

"Who is this? What's going on? "

"Sir, I'm going to need to talk to you. Can you tell me where you are, please?"

"What's going on? … Hello? … Hello?"

Jered was just saying, "Hello" for the third time when the front door opened again and a small, but wiry-looking police officer walked in, glanced quickly around the lobby and moved towards him. Jered looked up anxiously from his phone when the officer approached.

"Excuse me, sir, did you just receive a call?"

"Yes, I did. Can you tell me what this is all about?"

"Sir, I'm Officer Treadman, Phoenixville Police. I think we were just speaking on the phone."

Jered recognized the voice. "Yes, I think so."

[183]

"Can I ask what your name is?"

"My name is Jered Carr. But what –"

"Do you know a Benjamin Peterson?"

"Yes, I do. We're colleagues. What's happened?"

"I'm sorry to have to tell you, but Mr. Peterson's dead."

"Dead? How? What happened?"

"I'll explain in a moment, Mr. Carr. For right now, I need to ask you a few questions. Let's sit down somewhere."

Jered nodded dumbly and followed Treadman to an alcove near the lobby elevators where there was a small table flanked by two chairs. The two men sat down and Treadman began.

"I know this is going to be hard, Mr. Carr, but I need your help. Can you answer a few questions?"

"Yes – yes, of course," Jered finally found his voice.

"Good. Thanks. When was the last time that you talked to Mr. Peterson?"

"Uh, about forty minutes ago. He was in the ballroom with me and my wife and another colleague. We were getting ready to make a presentation. He left to go to the men's room before the presentation and he didn't come back. I – I don't know what happened after that. I figured he went up to his room or something. I was just calling him when – when you called me. How did he die? What happened?"

"We're still getting the details right now, Mr. Carr, but it seems Mr. Peterson fell from the balcony of his room."

"What? He wasn't drunk or anything. How could that have happened?"

"Like I said, we're still working on that. But we need your co-operation."

"Yes, of course."

"Do you know if Mr. Peterson was here with anyone?"

"You mean did he bring anyone?"

"That, or meet anyone here?"

"We all met before the party began. Ben, myself, my wife, Lauren, and our colleague Joel Williams."

"Are they still here?"

"Yes, they are. I can get them for you if you want." Jered was eager to do something. He'd half-risen to leave when Treadman said, "I'd appreciate that. If

you could just call them, maybe," Treadman
gestured towards Jered's phone.

"Right, of course." Jered sat slowly back down. It
had just occurred to him that this officer didn't trust
him. Well, why should he? They'd just met. Still, it
felt very strange to be treated with suspicion. He
sent a text to Lauren and in a few moments, she and
Williams appeared in the lobby.

Jered waved to them and they joined him and
Treadman. In a few low words, Jered explained
what had happened. The color drained from
Lauren's face as she heard the news. She stepped
back and caught her breath. Williams' eyes
narrowed, and his face hardened. Treadman said, "If
you three'll just come into the manager's office
with me, I'd like to hear what you can tell me about
this evening." Jered put a protective arm around his
wife and followed Treadman across the lobby
towards the manager's office. Williams brought up
the rear.

The manager's office had been turned into an
interview room. Treadman indicated a few chairs

placed outside the office door, and said, "Could you folks have seats for just a second?" The Carrs and Williams did as they were asked. Treadman peeked into the open office door and then nodded at Jered. "Could you go on in and tell Ranger Poole exactly what you just told me?" Jered nodded back and went in, closing the door behind him.

Williams asked, "Any idea how this happened?"

"We're trying to get answers to that. It's really pretty early to tell."

"Right, of course." Williams liked Treadman's response. He himself was on auto-pilot as he processed what was going on and he was grateful for this competent officer who seemed to be doing things right.

Jered Carr came out of the manager's office about ten minutes later. He said to his wife, "I think the detective wants to talk to you next." Lauren nodded and got up. She moved slowly into the office and shut the door. Jered watched her retreating back and slumped into the chair she'd just vacated. Williams asked, "You doing OK?"

"Yeah, it's just – hard when it's someone you know."

Williams nodded grimly. For a while the two men sat silent and staring. Then, Carr said, "What do you think happened?"

"I don't know." Williams shook his head. "Something just doesn't make sense."

Carr looked up at the tone of Williams' voice, but just then, the office door opened, and Lauren Carr came out.

"How'd it go?"

"It went OK," she said, nodding slowly. Williams got up to give her a seat and she smiled her thanks – a thin, forced smile.

Williams glanced at Treadman. "My turn?" he asked.

"Go on in."

Williams went into the manager's office. At the desk was Ranger Aaron Poole, the National Park Service Law Enforcement Ranger who'd been assigned to lead up this investigation. Since Peterson's death had taken place on Federal land at Valley Forge National Park, the National Park

Service had jurisdiction here. Poole was fifty-eight years old, clean-shaven, with light brown hair turning gray. When he saw Williams, he said, "Thanks for coming in. I'm Ranger Poole."

"I'm Joel Williams."

Poole turned the page of the legal pad on the desk to reveal a fresh sheet of paper. "OK, Mr. Williams. What can you tell me about this afternoon and evening?"

"Not as much as I'd like to, to be honest. I got here about four o'clock. I'd planned to meet with Ben – Ben Peterson – and Jered Carr at five-thirty. We met for a while and were ready to go with a presentation we were going to give for Second Chance's Information Night. They're holding it in the ballroom here at the hotel. Ben left the ballroom around six to go to the men's room. He never came back, and we were wondering what happened to him. Jered went out into the lobby to call him and he never picked up. That's all I know about today."

Poole was quick to notice the very slight emphasis on the last word. "Something else you think we should know?"

Williams looked at Poole for a long moment. Then he asked, "Did Jered Carr talk to you at all about our research study?"

Noticing Poole's reaction, Williams added, "I'm not trying to ask for any confidential information. It's just that I have a feeling that our research might be relevant to what happened to Ben, and I wanted to know if Jered brought it up at all."

"How about if you tell me about this research?" Williams was annoyed with himself. He should've known Poole wasn't going to tell him anything about what Jered had said. "OK, we've been conducting a study on Second Chance, focusing on their Cobbs Creek center. We're looking at all sorts of data to see just how effective the program is. And we found a few things we hadn't predicted."

Poole looked up expectantly from the notes he'd been taking.

"Such as?"

After a long pause, Williams said, "I don't want to raise the alarm if there's no reason to. You people have your hands full enough without that. But did you ever hear about a death a couple of years ago where a kid from the Cobbs Creek Second Chance Center fell off some scaffolding?"

"I vaguely remember hearing about that. Are you saying that's got something to do with Mr. Peterson's death?"

"That's just it. I don't know for sure. I only have an idea that it could be."

"What do you mean?"

Williams leaned forward in his chair. "Look, I can understand if you're skeptical about what I'm about to say. I might be, myself, in your shoes. I used to be a cop, so I know people can say all kinds of things."

Poole was interested. "You were a cop?"

"Yeah, in a place called Tilton, a couple of hours west of here."

Poole nodded, "Heard of it, actually. OK, so what is this connection you think there might be between a kid's death a couple of years ago and this death?"

"My team and I were taking a look at Cobbs Creek's history. You know, any background information we could find. We wanted to have an accurate picture of this program."

Poole nodded encouragingly.

[191]

"Ben was looking into the online news archives and found a story about this fifteen-year-old named Curtis Templeton who was a student at the Cobbs Creek Center. One day he snuck out to a construction site nearby, climbed up to the third floor and fell off some scaffolding."

"And you think there's something more to it, right?"

"Might be. I don't know for sure, and I don't want to jump to conclusions. But I do know this. The Second Chance people didn't want us to talk about the case in our presentation or discuss it in our paper."

"They can't have wanted the bad publicity."

"No, that's true. But to tell you the truth, we've had some questions about Curtis Templeton's death, and I'm getting the feeling we're being stonewalled."

Poole decided to get right to the point.

"It sounds like you think someone pushed that boy. Is that right? Why would anyone do that?"

"Don't know for sure. But do you mind if I tell you a sort of idea I have?"

"Go ahead."

"OK. Ben found some evidence that somebody at Second Chance might be skimming some money from the City. If Ben found out…"

Poole nodded slowly "…Maybe a student could have found out? Is that what you're saying?"

"I'm not saying that's how it did happen. But I think it could have. It would explain a lot, anyway."

"All right. I appreciate your telling us what you know."

Williams took the hint and straightened up to leave. When he'd gone, Poole tapped the pen he'd been using on the pad for moment or two. Then he picked up the hotel's house phone and spoke briefly into it. A few minutes later, there was a discreet knock on the door and the hotel manager came in. Poole looked up.

"Thanks for coming in."

"Of course. What can I do for you?"

"You've got a group of people here tonight from Second Chance, right?"

"That's right. They're having what they call Information Night. From what I understand, it's a mix-and-mingle event for investors and for city officials who might want to consider contracts with them."

"I want to talk to the Second Chance people. All of them. They're all still here, right?"

"Yes. I think their event is scheduled until ten-thirty, and I know several of them have booked rooms for the night."

"Good. I want to see all of them."

"I'll have my staff take care of it."

"Thanks."

Poole looked gratefully at the hotel manager's receding back. Nice to work with someone competent.

Jered and Lauren Carr sat miserably in the Riverton's bar, untouched glasses of cabernet in front of them. "I just can't believe it," Lauren said.

"I know. It really is, well, unbelievable."

"Jered, he *couldn't* have fallen. He had to have been pushed. That makes it ten times worse."

Jered looked across the table at his wife. "You really think someone pushed Ben?"

"Nothing else makes sense. He wouldn't have jumped, and I can't believe he fell." She looked anxiously back at him. "I didn't want to think so, but maybe Curtis Templeton was killed. Maybe the same person who did that is here – and killed Ben. Is that too crazy?"

Jered shook his head slowly, "I don't think so."

Lauren's eyes filled. "It's just hitting me. First that poor boy, and now Ben. What the hell is going on? This is all just…"

"…horrible," said Mark Donnelly. "Absolutely horrible! Of course, I didn't really know Ben Peterson. We talked a few times, but I couldn't tell you much about him."

"I understand," said Poole. "We're just trying to get a picture of what happened here this evening."

"Of course. Anything I can do to help."

"Thanks. Could you tell me a little about this whole Information Night event?"

"Sure. Every year we invite a group of people – investors, potential investors, city officials – to a hotel for a dinner and presentation. It's kind of a dog-and-pony show for our program, to be honest, but it's been successful. This year, we thought it'd

[195]

be a great idea to include Ben and his research team since they were doing a study of our program. We figured it'd lend us some more credibility and be good for the research team, too. I couldn't have imagined something like this would happen!"

"Let me get this all straight. You invited the research team tonight and they agreed. Do I have that right?"

"That's right."

"Anybody object?"

"Actually, no. Everyone thought it'd be terrific. Doesn't seem like such a good idea now," Donnelly said more quietly.

"And you got here at…."

"About five-thirty. I wanted all of the staff here early so that we could be ready."

"And then what happened?"

"I – let me think – I gave a little pep talk to the Second Chance people. You know, 'rah, team!' Then I talked for a few minutes with Ben, and Joel Williams, and Jered Carr. You should talk to them, too, if you haven't, by the way. They're the other researchers on the team. Anyway, then people started to come in and I was mingling. I was just wondering when the research team was going to get started when one of the hotel people came and got me and, well, you know the rest."

"Did you see Ben Peterson after you talked to the team?'

"No, not to speak to. I saw him from across the ballroom, but I got involved in a conversation and I didn't keep track of him after that."

"Got it. All right, that seems clear. Thanks, Mr. Donnelly. By the way, you've booked a room here for the night, right?"

"Yes, that's right."

"Good. I'll let you know if I have any more questions."

Donnelly didn't miss the note of dismissal in Poole's voice.

Outside the hotel, darkness had long since fallen. The temperature had dropped quickly, and a restless Joel Williams pulled his lightweight overcoat tighter as he walked across the hotel's parking lot. He had too much on his mind to stay in his room, and the bar would be too depressing. The only thing

Williams could think of to do was to walk. In a few moments, he'd reached the left side of the lot where Ben's body had fallen. Yellow police tape surrounded that part of the lot and two members of the local forensics unit were finishing up their work. One of them, a lanky young man with a military haircut and a navy blue "Forensics Unit" jacket, was holding a sheaf of plastic-wrapped papers in his hand.

"Can I help you?" he asked when he saw Williams.

"No," Williams answered. "Just taking a walk." The young man nodded and prepared to go back to work. Williams couldn't help noticing the papers in his hand – they looked like conference handouts. They must have been part of the crime scene – Williams didn't believe that Ben Peterson had jumped or fallen from that window – but that would mean Peterson had been holding them when he was pushed. If that were true, then that could be why Peterson went back to his room. He'd wanted to get handouts. The question was, who'd known where he was going?

"I'm afraid that's all I can tell you," Sheldon Adler said to Aaron Poole. "I got to the ballroom just before six, and I've been there ever since. I didn't even notice that Ben had left the ballroom. I was mingling with some of our investors and didn't really pay attention to what the research team was doing."

"Did you speak to Mr. Peterson at all?"

"Not one-to-one, no. A few of us from Second Chance were talking to the research team before the other guests started to come in, but that's the only time I spoke to Ben."

"What did you talk about?"

"Oh, Mark Donnelly – you've talked to him, right? – was just checking to make sure that the research team was ready to go."

"And were they?"

"Seemed to be."

"And you didn't see Mr. Peterson after that?"

"No. Like I said, I got busy mixing and mingling and didn't really pay any attention to the research team."

Poole made a note of Adler's hotel room number, thanked him for his time and ended the interview. Adler was the last member of the Second Chance staff to be interviewed, and none of them had seen Peterson after he left the ballroom. Poole rubbed his forehead and then the back of his neck. With a sigh, he straightened up, stretched and then radioed for Tracy Meyers, one of the two uniformed officers from nearby Phoenixville who'd been assigned to the scene. When Meyers arrived, Poole said, "Could you find out if anyone who was at this Information Night event saw Ben Peterson leave the ballroom?"

"Sure - Got it."

"Here's a list of the people who were here tonight. How about if you work with Treadman? Divide the list of names up and get contact information. Anybody saw anything or you think they might know something, I'd like to talk to 'em."

"OK."

Meyers left the room and Poole spent the next half hour reviewing what they knew about Ben Peterson's death. Peterson had seemed in good enough spirits when he'd arrived at the Riverton.

[200]

From what Poole had learned from Jered Carr, Peterson had been ready, along with the rest of the research team, to give the presentation. And yet, just a short while before it was to begin, he had ended up dead. Suicide was always possible – you never knew what was going on in people's lives until you looked a little deeper. But it didn't seem likely in this case. Accident too was possible but again, not likely. That meant someone hadn't wanted Ben to do his share of the presentation.

Poole's thoughts were interrupted by a tap on the door. It opened, and Meyers stuck her head in. "We've got a few people who saw Peterson leave the ballroom. Thought you'd want to know."

"Good. Send 'em in."

Meyers said, "OK. Here's the list of names."

"Thanks."

Five minutes later, the door opened again, and Therese Vaughan came in. Poole looked up.

"Thanks for coming in," he said. "You're…" he glanced down at the list, "Therese Vaughan?"

"That's right."

"You've heard about what happened here this evening?"

"Yes, it's just terrible! I'm afraid I can't be much help, though. I didn't know Ben Peterson very well or anything."

"Well, anything that you can tell us may be helpful. For instance, how did you come to be here tonight?"

"I work for the City of Philadelphia. I liaison with some of the programs and schools we contract with. Second Chance is one of those programs."

"Got it. And had you met Mr. Peterson before?"

"Just briefly. He and two other people were doing a study of Second Chance, I believe, and he asked a couple of questions about how the contracts work between the City and Second Chance."

"Did you see him here tonight?"

"Yes, he and the other researchers – at least I think that's who they were – were talking with Mark Donnelly and some of the Second Chance people when I got to the ballroom. Then some other people came, and I got to talking with someone else, and I didn't really get a chance to talk to any of the researchers."

"Did you see Mr. Peterson leave the ballroom?"

"Yes, I saw him leave about, oh, I guess it was six-fifteen or so. It's hard to say because I wasn't paying attention to the time."

"Was he with anyone?"

"No, not that I saw."

"And then what happened?"

"Well, then I got a glass of wine and got into another conversation and didn't see him again. I didn't even know what had happened until your officer came and told me."

"And there's nothing else you can tell me about Mr. Peterson?"

"No. Like I said, I barely knew him. We spoke briefly about their study – that's all."

Poole thanked Vaughan for her time. After she'd gone, he glanced at his watch. It was going to be a long night.

Chapter Nine

The next morning dawned cold and grayer than it had been the day before. It looked as though it was going to rain later and most of the Riverton guests who'd been at Information Night were eager to get going before it started. The Pennsylvania Turnpike and Schuylkill Expressway could be treacherous during a storm.

Aaron Poole and the two officers from Phoenixville had stayed up most of the night gathering their notes on Ben Peterson's death. Now, Poole was staring moodily at what they'd put together as he pushed his barely tasted breakfast around on his plate. He'd hoped somebody had seen Peterson talking to someone specific or going somewhere. That might at least have given him a clue to why the man had ended up face-down on the parking lot, four floors below his balcony. But nobody had seen much of anything. Typical. Well, he'd just have to wait to see what the forensics unit came up with. For now, he wanted to talk to that research team again. Nobody else seemed to really know Peterson at all, and you never knew what kind of resentments people might have when they worked closely together.

He drained his third cup of coffee, glanced at his watch and then left his room to go downstairs to the hotel manager's office where he and the team had set up a makeshift command center. On the way, he stopped at the reception desk and asked to have Jered and Lauren Carr and Joel Williams called.

Lauren Carr hung up the phone. "Jered, that police offer who interviewed us last night wants to talk to us again before we go."

"OK," her husband called from the bathroom. "I'll be ready in a minute." A few seconds later he appeared.

"I just can't get my mind around this whole thing," Jered said. "It seems so incredible."

"I know. I think I'm still in shock about it, myself. And I'm getting worried."

"What do you mean?"

"What if whoever killed Ben – and I'm sorry, I think he was killed – is going to try for you or me next?"

Jered's eyes dropped. "I have to admit. I was thinking the same thing. I don't want to be paranoid, though."

"No, but you and Joel Williams were working on that study, too. What if…?"

"Yeah, that's just it. 'What if?' Well, anyway, let's go down and see what that police officer wants."

Lauren nodded and the two left their room and went down the hall to the elevator.

When the door opened they saw that Joel Williams was inside. The three greeted each other.

"You don't look like you slept any better than we did," Jered said

"I didn't. This whole thing is…"

"Yeah."

"Joel," Lauren said. "You used to be a cop. What do you think? Ben was murdered, right? Just like Curtis Templeton."

"Too early to say for sure," Williams responded. "But I wouldn't be surprised."

Lauren looked up at the tone in his voice. "You think those two deaths might be connected?"

"I can't say for sure. Not yet, anyway. But I've got an idea they might be."

Jered looked unhappily at Joel. "I can't say I'm shocked to hear you say that. We've all had the feeling that something's wrong."

Just then, the elevator doors opened, and the three passengers exited. By unspoken agreement, they didn't discuss the murder as they crossed the hotel lobby to the manager's office. When they got there, Williams tapped on the doorframe of the opened office door and Poole looked up from the papers he'd been holding.

"Thanks for coming down. Come on in and have seats."

The three took seats and Poole began.

"We're trying to piece together what happened to your friend last night. I know I've talked to you already, but I've got a couple more things I'd like to follow up on."

"Whatever we can do," Lauren murmured. Jered nodded his agreement.

"Of course," Joel said.

"Good. It looks like Mr. Peterson left the ballroom at about six-fifteen. Does that sound right?"

"I guess so," Jered said. "I can't be sure, though."

"And none of you saw him after that?"

"No, we didn't," Joel said. "He said he'd be back soon, and he knew we were supposed to present right after the dinner."

"Right," Lauren said, "And that was supposed to start at seven."

"So, Mr. Peterson said he was going to the restroom, and that he'd be right back. Anyone know why he went up to his room?"

"I think it was to get some handouts," Joel said. "He'd made some handouts for our presentation, and I guess he forgot them in his room. He probably went back upstairs for them."

"He didn't say anything about them to you?"

"No, but he was the one with the presentation information – the PowerPoint slides, that kind of thing. I'm pretty sure he'd have made handouts, and I know he didn't have them when we first met."

[208]

"OK, and you three were all in the ballroom the whole time?"

"That's right," Jered said.

"Anyone in particular who saw you there?"

All of a sudden, it struck Jered that he and Lauren were under suspicion. Joel, too. He glanced at the others; it was clear that they'd had the same thought. Slowly, his face draining of some of its color, he said, "You think one of us could have – could have killed Ben?"

"To be honest, I don't think anything right now. I'm just trying to get as much information as I can. You three knew Mr. Peterson, probably better than anyone else here." The implication wasn't lost on anyone.

"I know you have to ask this kind of question," Joel finally said. "It's just hard to feel like you're under suspicion. Especially when it's a friend. "

"I can imagine," Poole said. "But like you said, I have to ask some questions that aren't very nice to ask. And honestly, I'd like nothing better than for somebody to verify that all of you were in the ballroom the whole evening. Is there anyone who could?"

[209]

Joel thought for a moment and then snapped his fingers. "Got it! We were working with one of the hotel's technicians, setting up everything for the presentation. I'll bet she'd be willing to verify that we were all there when Ben died."

"You get her name?"

"No, I'm sorry I forget that. Either of you remember?" Both Carrs shook their heads.

"OK. I can ask the hotel manager about that." Poole made some notes. Then he put his pen down and looked up at the three people in front of him. "Can any of you add anything else? Anything that can help us understand what happened would be helpful."

The three sat silent for a moment. Then Lauren spoke up. "I didn't want to believe it at first. But I'm glad you're investigating this. I think Ben was murdered."

"That what you two think, too?" Poole asked.

"I don't like it, but, yeah, I do," Jered said.

"I think so, too," Joel added.

"Fair enough. And you," Poole looked at Williams "think it has something to do with this research study your team was doing. Is that right?"

"That's right."

Both of the Carrs glanced at Williams. Then Jered said, "It sure seems that way. We'd found some things out that the Second Chance people couldn't have been happy about. In fact, maybe I'm being paranoid, but I think they were worried we were going to say too much last night about what we'd found."

"Does any of you have a copy of that presentation you were going to make?"

"Ben had the slides," Williams said. "But I have an outline if that'll help."

"It might. Let's see it."

Williams opened the briefcase he'd been carrying and pulled out a sheet of paper. He glanced at it to be sure it was the right paper and then handed it to Poole, who nodded his thanks. Poole took a quick look at it and then said "I know we talked about this a little last night, but tell me again. What is it about this research that you think was so much of a problem for Second Chance?"

Williams answered first this time. "Well, like I said last night, Ben found out that a student who attended Second Chance's Cobbs Creek center died two years ago. Nobody's saying much about it. Everyone says it was an accident, and the way it looks on the surface, it could have been. But then we found out something else – about the Cobbs Creek attendance records."

"That's right," Jered added. "Ben found out that the attendance records at Cobbs Creek and the City were different from the records at Second Chance's headquarters."

Lauren put in, "And that makes a big difference in funding. The City funds programs like Second Chance based partly on attendance. The more attendance, the more funding."

"OK," Poole said, "I think I understand. And I appreciate your telling me this. It's going to be really helpful."

"Is it best if we stay here, or can we head back to Horsham?" Jered asked when they were done.

"I don't think there's anything else I need to ask you just now. Just make sure the contact information I have for you is right."

All three did so and when they'd verified what they saw, they got up to leave.

After a few more questions, Poole ended the interview in what Joel Williams thought was a fairly smooth and professional way. He'd done plenty of interviews himself, and he respected the way Poole was going about it.

"Thanks," Poole said as they left. "We'll be in touch."

After they'd gone, Poole shuffled again through the notes he'd been able to gather about Ben Peterson. There wasn't much, really. They'd have to dig into his background more and see if that led anywhere. He'd check out those researchers and make sure they'd been where they said they were. Then he'd get onto the lead they'd had given him and see what he could find out. But you always started close to home.

Mark Donnelly steered his Audi carefully into the traffic on the winding road that led from the Riverton to Second Chance's headquarters. The rain had started and although his car generally handled the road well, he didn't want to take chances and you never knew what other drivers would do. Besides, he needed to figure out what to do next. One thing was for sure; he was going to have to do damage control starting as soon as he got to the office. He'd expected last night to go without a hitch. He should've known better. Who knew what would now be blazed across the Internet and mentioned in newscasts? He'd have to have to take some quick action if he was going to keep things from spinning completely out of control.

After twenty minutes, Donnelly had arrived at the headquarters building and parked in his reserved spot in the parking garage. He took the elevator straight from the garage to the third floor and was soon settled into his office chair. The first order of business was to make sure that everyone was on the same page about what they'd tell the press. Donnelly called an emergency meeting of his staff.

When everyone had assembled in the third-floor conference room, he began the meeting.

"Thanks for coming. As you all know, Information Night is an important way for us to connect with school systems, City authorities and other folks who are interested in working with us to give our kids a chance. The Riverton Hotel hosted us last night, and we're all really grateful to the hotel staff. They did a great job. Tragically, though, there was a terrible accident at the hotel while we were there."

There were a few shocked gasps and murmurs of "Oh, my God!" After a moment, Donnelly continued:

"Let me assure you that nobody who works for Second Chance was hurt or even involved in the accident, but, unfortunately, one of the hotel guests died while we were there. So, you might get calls about it. If you do, just refer the caller to my office. The authorities haven't released a lot of details, so there's not much more I can tell you. But I didn't want you to hear any garbled facts or misinformation. Now, does anyone have any questions?"

There was silence as everyone digested what Connelly had said. After a moment or two, he ended the meeting with a final remark:

"Thanks again, everyone. If any questions come up, please come let me know."

Lauren Carr slowly left the conference room with the rest of the staff. Absorbed in thought, she didn't notice Donnelly watching her as she went. The more she thought about it, the more certain she was now that Ben had been murdered. Did Mark Donnelly have something to do with it? Lauren didn't want to believe it. She'd worked with Donnelly for five years and had come to respect him. She'd always thought of him as dedicated to the Second Chance students and their families. But he'd been there last night. And he'd just flat-out lied to the staff. Now she simply didn't know what to think any more. In this distracted state, she reached her office and unlocked the door. She almost jumped when she heard a voice behind her.

"Can I talk to you for a minute, Lauren?"

"Yeah, sure," she replied, flicking her office light on.

Mark Donnelly followed her into the office and sat down in one of her functional but not particularly luxurious office chairs.

When Lauren had sat down at her desk chair, Donnelly said,

"You must be really upset about what happened last night."

"Yeah, I am."

"Look, I know it may sound harsh, but we don't really know what happened to Ben. For us to let wild rumors get around would be a big mistake and I know you wouldn't want that, would you?"

"No, of course not."

"Good. Glad we're on the same page about this. I really think it's best to just let the police handle everything. In the meantime, it's not going to help anything if there's too much talk. I think it'd be best if we just try to get back to normal and focus on doing our best for the Second Chance kids. Make sense?"

"I guess so."

"All right, then." Donnelly gave her an awkward and somehow appealing smile. "Look, I'm not insensitive. I'm just trying to do the best I can. This isn't easy for any of us."

Lauren nodded. "I know," she said.

Donnelly said, "See you later. I'll be in my office if you need me."

"OK"

Ranger Aaron Poole sat at his desk at the Valley Forge Park Support Station, looking again through his notes on the Ben Peterson case. He'd spent the last few hours starting to put together some of the pieces of Peterson's life. So far what he'd found out hadn't been particularly helpful. A check of the criminal justice databases he had access to had shown nothing for Peterson. He'd made a call to an ex-girlfriend who'd moved to Delaware and now worked for the Delaware State Police and asked her to run a check in that state. Not much there, either – just a couple of speeding tickets. The next step would be to try to find out find out more from the people who'd known and worked with Peterson at Caesar Rodney College. That would mean a trip to Delaware. And there was that lead he'd gotten from those researchers about Second Chance. After he'd talked with them, he'd talked again to the hotel manager and gotten the name of the technician they'd worked with for their presentation. Her story backed up what they'd said. Of course, you never could be completely sure, but it looked like none of them could have pushed Peterson over that balcony. And what the researchers had told him about Second Chance was an interesting possibility, especially considering that a bunch of company representatives had been at the hotel that night. Poole decided that the best thing to do would be to divvy up the work. There was no way he could do it all anyway, given how thinly stretched the staff at Valley Forge was. He was trying to figure out what he was going to do when a voice said, "Looks you got a lot going on there."

Poole looked up to see his boss, Chief Ranger Paul Bigelow, a rugged-looking man who'd spent most of his life outdoors and still at the age of sixty-two went rock climbing whenever he got the chance. "Sorry," Poole said, "I didn't know you were coming by today."

"I heard what happened last night and I wanted to see what needs to be done."

"Plenty, actually. I'm just getting started here. Got a long way to go."

"Let's see what you got so far." Bigelow took a seat on the other side of Poole's spare wooden desk and, together the two began to go over the information Poole had and notes that he'd made on Ben Peterson's death.

After about half an hour, it was clear to both men that this investigation could get complicated.

"There's the Philadelphia angle – the Second Chance center in Cobbs Creek – and then there's the Valley Forge angle. Then, we need to find out what we can from Delaware," Poole summarized.

"You need some help on this?"

"That's just it. There is nobody. You know that as well as I do."

"We could work with the State Police."

"Yeah, I know. I might end up needing to do that, but I'd rather find a simpler way of coordinating it all. The fewer organizations involved in this, the easier it is."

"That's the truth. But we're going to need to get this cleared up soon. I've got some other meetings now, but I'll be back later this afternoon. How about you work out what kind of help you're going to need and where, and let me know then, OK? We'll try to figure out how we're going to get it done."

"Thanks, I will."

Therese Vaughan pulled into the tiny parking lot of the Maplewood School near Philadelphia's Logan Square. She hadn't seen her Nicole since yesterday afternoon when she'd dropped the child off to spend the night with her cousins. That was always a treat for Nicole, but it didn't make Therese feel much less guilty about leaving her. Just as well they'd made those plans, though, with everything going on. Therese sat in the car for a moment, just trying to absorb it all. She didn't want to think about the way Ben Peterson had died or about the way that cop had kept asking her questions. She'd answered them well enough, anyway. Nobody could say she'd done badly. Still, it shook her up. She was going to have figure out what to do from here, especially if there were any more questions. That was going to have to wait, though. For now, she had a lunch date with her little girl. And after all, that was the only thing that mattered. Her face brightened as she got out of the car and walked towards the school with the heels of her new pumps clacking purposefully on the pavement.

Sheldon Adler sifted through his mail. One letter in particular caught his eye and he opened it with a not-very-muffled curse. Not again! That skunk of a lawyer that Valerie had hired was trying to get more money! This was the third time in a year that Valerie and her attorney had taken Adler to court about their divorce settlement. Adler had no idea how he would have paid the outrageous settlement the court had originally given Valerie if he hadn't figured out a way to take care of matters. And even that wasn't enough for that bitch. Now he was going to have to get his own lawyer involved again. At the rate Valerie was going, he might as well try to find out what his lawyer would charge for a retainer.

Aaron Poole finished organizing what would need to be done for the Peterson investigation. The way he saw it, he could handle the Second Chance headquarters part of it without much trouble; the headquarters wasn't far. It wouldn't be as easy to do the Philadelphia and Delaware parts of the job, though. What he needed was a liaison. Someone who could help tie together those parts of this case. Someone who knew the people involved and could help him connect the dots. Well, he could at least start by trying to find someone in the Philadelphia Police Department he could talk to about Second Chance of Cobbs Creek. Then he remembered something one of the researchers had told him. Something about knowing someone on the Philadelphia police force. A quick glance at his notes reminded him of the name – Joel Williams.

Joel Williams had dismissed his Senior Seminar class and returned to his office. He was looking forward to an hour of peace and quiet to start working on his students' paper proposals. More than almost any other class he taught, Williams found that his Senior Seminar class took up a lot of his reading time. He put on the reading glasses he'd recently begun using and picked up the first proposal. Five minutes later he was interrupted by a tap on his open office door. He looked up to see Shirley Mizzello standing at his open office door.

"Shirley, hi,"

"Is this a bad time?" It was, but Williams felt guilty about not having kept up with the latest on the new center.

"No, it's fine. Come on in."

"Thanks." Mizzello took a seat across from Williams' desk. "I'm glad you're here. We've managed to get an appointment with the dean, and I hope you can be there."

"When's the meeting?'

"Friday at nine. You free?"

Williams checked his online calendar. "Looks like it."

Mizzello's face brightened up. "Glad to hear it. We really need to support us on this, Joel. I'll send you the information we put together, so you can read it before we meet."

"All right, thanks."

Mizzello thanked him again and left. Williams looked up at the ceiling for a moment. The one thing he didn't need was a political fight in the School of Social Sciences.

The buzz of his office telephone interrupted his thoughts.

"Criminal Justice. Joel Williams speaking."

"Dr. Williams? This is Aaron Poole, Valley Forge National Park Service. Do you have a couple of minutes?"

"Sure," Williams promptly forgot about the center and about the pile of proposals on his desk. "What can I do for you?"

"We're working on figuring out what happened to your colleague, Ben Peterson, and I've got a question for you. Remember you told me that you knew somebody on the Philadelphia police force?"

"Of course."

"Can you give me his name and number? I'd like to get in touch with him."

"Sure, just give me a minute."

Poole waited while Williams opened up his electronic address book and found the entry for Carter Barclay.

"OK," Williams said. "His name is Carter Barclay, and he's at the 19th District in Philadelphia." Then, he gave Poole Barclay's telephone number.

Poole read the name and number back to Williams and then thanked him.

"Anything else I can do?" Williams asked. "Ben was a friend. I'd like to do whatever I could."

"Not for right now, thanks. I'll give you a call back if anything else comes up."

"I'd appreciate it."

When Poole had finished his conversation with Williams, he called Carter Barclay.

"19th District, Barclay."

"Detective Barclay? My name is Aaron Poole. I'm a Law Enforcement Ranger up at Valley Forge."

"What can I do for you?"

"Well, last night, we had a death up here at the Riverton Hotel. One of the people who knew the victim is someone who says he knows you. You know a Joel Williams?"

"Joel Williams? Sure. He and I have been friends for a while. We worked together in the Tilton Police Department."

"You know him well?"

"Pretty well, yeah. Wait – is there some kind of problem?"

"Not really, I don't think. Just checking up on some things. He ever mention a man named Ben Peterson?"

"I don't think so. Why?"

"That's the name of the person who died last night. Apparently, he was working on a research project with Dr. Williams and another person."

"Oh, you mean the Second Chance project? Joel told me about that."

"Do you mind telling me what he told you about it?"

"Well, he told me they were doing a study of Second Chance. He also asked me about a Second Chance kid who died down here a couple of years ago."

"Curtis Templeton?"

"Yeah, that's the one. He tell you about that, too?"

"Yeah, he did. Listen, I have an awkward question to ask you. Do you trust Williams?"

"Absolutely. He and I were partners. I trusted him with my life then and I would now, too."

Poole thought for a long minute. An idea had occurred to him. It would be a risk, but it would be worth taking, he thought. Then he said, "Would you be willing to co-operate with me on something?"

"Depends what, but go ahead."

"OK. I've got this death up here. We're spread kind of thin and I could use some help with this case. You're a cop, and Williams was a cop. You know the routine and between you, you know the people involved. I could use someone like Williams who can work with the different police departments and talk to some people. Do some liaising, too. And I could use your help, too, since Williams is a civilian. And to be honest, he's connected with this. If Williams is willing, would you work with him?"

"Yeah, why not. It'd be nice to team up again."

"Fantastic. I'll call him and if he's willing, we'll see if we can get this going."

"Works for me."

As soon as he'd gotten off the phone with Barclay, Poole called Williams back. Once they'd greeted each other, Poole made the same proposition to Williams as he'd made to Barclay.

Williams thought about it. He was in the middle of a semester, and doing this consulting would mean a lot of traveling. But then he thought of Ben Peterson and realized that he really had no choice. Besides, it would be good to be in touch with Carter again and work with him.

"Let me talk to my wife and call you back. That OK?"

"Yeah, of course. Whatever you need to do. But I'd like to get started on this as soon as we can. You know how it is…"

"…The first couple of days matter the most."

"Exactly."

"Not a problem. I'll call you back before the end of the day."

"Thanks."

Twenty minutes later, Bigelow stopped back in to Poole's small office area. "So, how's it going?" he asked Poole.

"I think I have an idea…" Poole responded.

Jered Carr noticed that Lauren had been unusually quiet at dinner, as though she were thinking something over. "What's on your mind?" he asked.

"I just can't get over what's happened, Jered. It's all just so horrible."

"It is," he said, nodding.

"But there's more, Jered. You don't know. Today, I was at this meeting that Mark Donnelly had. He glossed over the whole thing as though it had nothing to do with Second Chance. Then after the meeting, he came to my office and basically told me to keep my mouth shut. He didn't use those words, but that's the message I got."

"So, you think Mark Donnelly might have something to do with this?"

"I don't know, Jered. I'm not a cop. I just don't know what to think anymore. I never would have thought Mark Donnelly was the type of person to cover things up, but you should have heard him today – all hush-hush, 'think of the kids' and 'yay team.' I'm just upset about it."

Jered took a sip of the beer he'd had with dinner. "I'm wondering if it would be a good idea to maybe tell somebody about this."

"I'm thinking about that, too. I don't know whether I'm being paranoid or not. Probably I am. But I just – I want to know what happened to Ben. I don't want to accuse Mark of anything, but it was creepy the way he tried to pass this whole thing off."

"Well, there is that cop we talked to last night. He gave us his number and if you want, we could call him."

"Yeah, maybe I'll do that."

Chapter Ten

Mark Donnelly had just sat down at his desk the next morning and turned his computer on when Grace Wong stuck her head in the door. "Ranger Aaron Poole from Valley Forge Park Services is here to see you."

"Oh, thanks. Send him in, please."

Donnelly rose to greet Poole as he entered the office. "Nice to see you again. Have a seat. What can I do for you?"

"Thanks," Poole took a seat on one of the simple but plush chairs opposite Donnelly's own desk chair. "I'm really hoping you can help me out with some questions I have about Ben Peterson's death."

"Of course. Anything I can do."

"Thanks. Now, from what I've learned, Mr. Peterson was doing a study of Second Chance, is that right?"

"Exactly. He and his team had been looking at how successful Second Chance students are as compared to those who are in other programs, and to students who don't have access to alternative programs. We were really excited about the study, too."

"Sounds like they found some positive results."

"Well, you'll have to talk to them about exact numbers and that kind of thing. We hadn't gotten to see their preliminary results and now, well…."

"I understand."

"But I do know that they'd found that kids in our programs are less likely to go through the juvenile justice system and more likely to finish high school than those who aren't in the program."

"That does sound good."

"It is. But like I said, you'll have to talk to the other researchers about the details."

"That's a good idea. Since I'm here anyway, do you mind if I ask you a couple of questions about what you folks do here at the headquarters?"

"Sure, of course."

"Now, you're the 'nerve center,' right?"

"Pretty much. Each center – we have three right now, and hopefully more on the way – has a director and an assistant director who manage everything at the center level. They're the ones who interact with the students, work with families and do the day-to-day decision-making. But we do the big-picture hiring, budgeting and so on."

[233]

"Got it. So, I guess that means you do a lot of traveling around to the centers."

"Me? Sometimes. But we use a lot of technology, too, to keep in touch. We have online meetings, our reports get sent electronically and of course, there's always the telephone,"

"So, if I wanted to know what's happening at Cobbs Creek, for instance, there'd be reports right here that would give me information?"

"Well, you'd have to talk to them down there about individual students and daily schedules and that kind of thing. But the big picture information is here."

"That makes sense. Now, each center sends you a weekly report or something? Is that how it works?"

"Some reports are weekly, like each center's discipline incident summary and some overall progress reports. But a lot of the reports are monthly. Budgets, grades, attendance, that kind of thing, are all done monthly."

"I think I understand. Could I see a few of those reports? It'll help me make more sense of the way things work."

"Of course. Any reports in particular?"

"Could I see this past month's reports for Cobbs Creek?"

"You mean the weekly and monthly reports?"

"If you don't mind."

"It'll take a few minutes, but I can get them for you."

"I'd appreciate it."

Donnelly buzzed for his assistant and when she arrived, he asked her for the reports he'd promised Poole. While they waited, Donnelly asked, "Can I get you anything? Coffee? Tea? A soda?"

"No, nothing, thanks."

The two men waited in silence. Poole glanced around the office, taking note of the simple but top-quality furnishings and the tailored cut of Donnelly's suit. No expense spared here.

When Donnelly's assistant returned with the copies, both men thanked her and after flipping through the papers to be sure they were the right ones, Donnelly handed them to Poole.

"Thanks," Poole said.

"Of course. Anything else I can do?"

"I don't want to take up any more of your time this morning. I know you're busy. This is just what I need to get started."

"Glad to help. Let me know if anything else comes up."

"Thanks, I will."

As Poole left Donnelly's office and went down the hall away from it, he could feel Donnelly watching him.

Poole's next stop was Lauren Carr's office. When he got there, he saw that she wasn't in it, and settled down to wait. This office wasn't nearly as nicely appointed as Donnelly's, but she kept it neat. Mostly books, binders, that kind of thing. He was just getting a feel for the office and for Lauren when she came in.

"I'm sorry," she said, "I didn't know you were here. I hope you haven't been waiting long."

"No, not at all. I was here anyway and thought I might as well kill two birds with one stone."

Lauren went slowly around behind her desk and sat down. "I'm glad you did. I was going to call you, actually."

Poole waited expectantly. He'd often found that simply sitting quietly was enough to get people to talk, and he wasn't disappointed.

"I'm concerned about something, and I don't know if I should make a big deal about it or not."

"How about if you tell me, and we can figure out whether it's something we should make a big deal about?"

Lauren paused and then nodded. "OK, but – well – I think I'd be more comfortable talking about it somewhere else. There's a coffee shop in a little strip plaza about two blocks away."

"All right."

Lauren put on the lightweight coat she'd worn that morning and picked up her purse. Then she and Poole left the office and took the elevator down to the street level. They left the building and were soon seated at a booth in The Bay Tree, a small café that served gourmet coffees and teas. It wasn't Poole's kind of place, but it was the closest place where they could sit down and talk outside of Lauren's office.

Once they'd ordered their coffee, paid and sat down, Poole said, "So there was something you wanted to talk to me about."

Lauren nodded and looked out the window as she gathered her thoughts. "It's about a guy I work with – one of my bosses. You must have met him at the Riverton. He was there. His name's Mark Donnelly."

Poole nodded. No need yet for her to know he'd just talked to Donnelly. "I remember meeting him."

"Well, I'm really beginning to wonder about him. Yesterday we had an emergency staff meeting about Ben's death. He just glossed over everything, as though Ben's dying had nothing to do with Second Chance."

"And you think it does."

"Yes, like I told you the other night. But what's worse is that later, after the meeting, Mark came to my office and basically told me to keep my mouth shut and not say anything to anyone and just let it go. It seems like he's hiding something."

"Any idea what that might be?"

Lauren looked up at him with dismay in her eyes. "I don't know for sure, and I don't want to throw accusations around. But it might be about the study that Ben and Jered and Joel Williams were doing. Jered and Joel told you about that, right?"

"I've heard about it, yeah."

"Well, they found some attendance records that just didn't make sense. We talked about it and we think somebody might have been padding the records. The city pays Second Chance based on attendance, so the more students on the attendance records, the more Second Chance gets paid."

"I understand what you're saying. And you think Mr. Donnelly knew about this?"

"That's the thing. I don't know whether he knew or not and I'm not accusing him of anything. I honestly don't know what to think anymore."

"All right, let's leave it like this. The research team found out that the attendance records might be padded. Anybody who was responsible for that padding wouldn't want it to be discovered. Do I have it right so far?"

"Right."

"OK, good. Thanks for what you've told me. Every piece of information we get can be helpful. And don't worry," Poole responded to Lauren's worried expression, "everything you say is completely confidential. Nobody needs to know it came from you."

"Thanks." Lauren's expression brightened. She glanced at her watch and said, "Sorry, but I've got to get back to the office."

"Not a problem. I should get a move on, too. Call me if you think of anything else I should know."

"I will." With that, Lauren lifted her coat from the back of the chair she'd been sitting in and picked up her bag. Then she left the café with a murmur of thanks.

Joel Williams had spent yesterday afternoon with Ed Beaumont, arranging to be away from campus a few days a week.

"You'll be there for Wednesday's meeting, won't you," Ed asked. "It's pretty important."

"I know. I've got it on my calendar."

This morning, he'd met with Alicia Cardenas to get final approval for his change of schedule.

"It won't be a problem," Alicia said as she signed the approval document. Then she said, "I'm actually glad you stopped in. I've got a meeting in a few

[240]

minutes, but I want to set up a time to talk to you about a new initiative we're working on. You'll be here on Friday morning, right?"

"That's right. In fact –"

"Of course. You're coming in anyway with Shirley Mizzello and her group, aren't you?"

"Exactly."

"Well, why don't you stay for a few minutes after that meeting, and you and I can chat. Does that work?"

Williams nodded. "That'll work fine," he said.

"Good," Cardenas said. "I'm counting you to be a part of this initiative. You've been doing research on that for-profit alternative school, right? That's the background we need. But we'll talk more about it on Friday."

Williams took his cue and soon left.

He thought about what Cardenas' new initiative might be during the drive to Philadelphia. Most likely it was the new center she'd announced. If it was, he wasn't at all sure he was enthusiastic about it. Shirley Mizzello was right about the whole question of curriculum design and implementation.

Faculty should be doing that. And if this new center would change that, Williams would have a problem with it.

When he got to Cobbs Creek, Williams parked his Dodge sedan at a curb space he'd been lucky enough to find only two blocks from the Second Chance center. He didn't have class again until the next day, and he would announce revised office hours to his students then. For now, he wanted to talk with Sheldon Adler. Adler had on-the-spot knowledge about what happened at the Cobbs Creek center and he'd known both Ben and Curtis Templeton.

Williams got to the school, signed in and was asked to wait a few minutes until Adler was free. A short time later, Adler came into the main office where Williams was waiting and greeted him.
"I'm glad you came by. I'm just so sorry about what happened to Ben Peterson!"
"Thanks. It's a shock, that's for sure."
"I'm sure it is. It's just terrible. So, what can I do for you?"

"Well, Jered Carr and I talked it over and we would really like to go ahead and finish the study we've been working on, even without Ben."

"I was wondering what you folks were going to decide to do about that."

"We were, too, at first. But it's a sound study, and we figured that if what we found could help some students, too, so much the better."

"Well, I think that's great. How can I help?"

"I know you'd talked to Ben several times and given him a lot of help. Do you think we could go over a few things, just so I have it all straight?"

"Sure. Let's go back to my office."

The two men went back to Adler's office where they sat down. Then Adler said, "OK, what would you like to go over?" For a few minutes, he and Williams reviewed a few points about school policy. Then Williams broached the real topic he wanted to discuss.

"Now, Ben told us that you keep attendance records here at the center and at headquarters. Is that right?"

"Right."

"Well, I guess that's what's confusing me. We found that the attendance records at the center didn't match what we got from headquarters. Remember we said something about that at Information Night?"

"Right, of course. I don't know if Ben got the chance to tell you, but I think that was just some kind of glitch – the last page left off of a document or something. You know how it is when you try to send things electronically."

"So, the records we should use for our study are the ones that are here?"

"That's right."

"Good, that answers that question. I'd also like to understand a little better how your accreditation works. You send everything to the City of Philadelphia, and they're the ones who establish the contracts with Second Chance, right?"

"Well, we're accredited by the Middle States Association of Colleges and Schools. But we're contracted by the City to provide educational services."

"Got it. That's what I thought. And I know Ben had talked with your contact at the City, too."

"Therese Vaughan. Yes, I'm pretty sure he talked to her, and I'm sure she'd be happy to talk to you, too."

"I'd appreciate that. I'm sure I'm going to want to chat with her at some point."

"That's good. Is there anything else you need from me right now?

"Not at the moment. Would it be OK if I call you if something comes up?"

"Sure, that's fine."

Just then, Adler's office phone rang. He held up one finger to ask Williams to wait and answered the call. The call was from a parent, though, and Adler soon guessed that this would take some time. He put the caller on hold and excused himself to Williams.

"Sorry, but I really need to take this call and I'll be a few minutes."

"Oh, that's no problem at all. I can find my way out. I'll let you know if I need anything."

"Thanks. And thanks for coming in."

Williams nodded his own thanks and left Adler's office.

When Williams got back to the main office, he signed out and thanked Martine Roberts, who glanced up and smiled in acknowledgement. Then, her face clouded over, and she said, "Look, it's none of my business, but I was sorry to hear about your friend."

"Thanks. They told you about that?"

"Word gets around. You know how it is."

"Yeah, I know."

Lowering her voice a little, she said, "One of my friends works up at headquarters. She heard it up there."

Williams took his chance. "I heard you had something like that happen here a couple of years ago."

Martine's eyes dropped. "Yeah. Curtis Templeton. A pain in the butt sometimes but not a bad kid. I liked him. He worked here, you know."

"I thought he was a student."

"No, I mean he worked here with me in the main office. That was his job that he did. All the kids have jobs they do besides their classes. Supposed to teach them responsibility."

"Did he do a good job?"

"Yeah. In fact, he was working here the day he, well, you know, died. He was doing stuff for me in the morning, then later in the day we heard about what happened to him. Freaked me out."

"I'll bet it did," Williams said sympathetically. "What did he do for you here?"

"Well, he filed stuff, stapled handouts, put the mail in the staff mailboxes, that kind of thing."

"I'll bet you miss having his help."

"I liked him, yeah. I've got Patrice to help me now, though, and she's a good worker. Not so much of a mouth on her, either, if you know what I mean."

"I know what you mean."

Martine glanced at her watch, and Williams took the hint. "I'll let you get back to work," he said. Martine smiled and Williams left. He barely noticed anything as he walked back towards his car. He was processing what Martine Robertson had told him. Curtis Templeton had worked in the main office. He could easily have seen attendance records. If he was reasonably bright, there was no reason he couldn't have noticed the difference in the number of names at some point. That would certainly make a connection between his death and Ben's.

Carter Barclay was looking forward to a day off the next day. He'd been working on a new Gangs Unit initiative that the City was putting together, and it was taking up more time than he'd thought it would. It'd be worth it, though, if the top brass would only pay attention to what the regular detectives said and set up a realistic program. He was about to clean his desk up and leave for the day when his phone rang.

"19th District, Barclay."

"Detective Barclay? It's Aaron Poole."

Despite his strong desire for a very hot shower followed by a very cold beer, Barclay's interest was piqued.

"How are you?"

"I'm doing well. I just wanted to ask if I could take a look at whatever you've got on that Curtis Templeton case we talked about. See if I can find anything in it that's a link to this case."

"Let me see what I can come up with and email you what I have. What's your email address?"

Poole gave him the information and thanked him.

[248]

Joel Williams paused at Therese Vaughan's open office door, and then knocked on the frame. She looked up, and, after a second, she recognized him. "Come on in" she said.

"Thanks." Williams took a seat on one of the straight-backed black office chairs that faced her desk.

"Thanks for seeing me on such short notice," he began. "I know you're busy."

"Not a problem," she said. "I have a meeting in about half an hour, though, just so you know."

"I won't take up that much time. Promise." Williams smiled at her. He'd learned on the police force, and while serving on more than one university committee, how to be affable when it suited his purpose. "It's about the study of Second Chance that my colleague Ben Peterson – you met him, right? – and I were working on with another colleague."

"Oh, yes, of course. So terrible about Ben!"

"Thanks. We're all pretty upset about it. "

"And so sudden, too! I was talking to him that night at the Riverton and then, well…"

"Oh, you got the chance to talk to him?"

"Well, only for a bit. He was on his way through the hotel lobby and it looked like he was in a hurry. But he seemed fine. And then it was almost no time at all before we heard he was dead."

"It did happen quickly. We're still in shock. But we decided to go ahead and finish the original study."

"I'm happy for you. That can't have been an easy decision."

"It wasn't, but I think it's the right one. Second Chance is a good program, and it deserves to get some press. That's why I'm here."

"I think it's a good program, too."

"You've been working with Second Chance for a couple of years now, haven't you?"

"That's right. For four years now."

"So, you probably heard about it back a couple of years ago when one of the students – Curtis Templeton was his name – died, didn't you?"

"Oh, that was just terrible. I didn't know the boy myself. But everybody at the Cobbs Creek Center was all broken up about it."

"I'm sure they were. Is that how you found out about it? Someone from the Center?"

"I had a meeting over there that afternoon. And when I got there, they – told me what had happened."

Williams' face didn't show it – he'd had too much experience as a detective for that – but he tuned in intently to what Therese Vaughan said. She had been at Second Chance of Cobbs Creek on the day Curtis Templeton had died. He chose his next words carefully.

"So, you go out to the different Second Chance centers?"

"Sometimes. I do an initial visit during the contract approval process, and then I make periodic visits to the centers."

"And that day was your day to visit Cobbs Creek?"

"That's right. I was supposed to have a meeting with Tim Dawson, the Cobbs Creek director, and Sheldon Adler. But when I got there, I found out the meeting had to be cancelled because of, well, because of what had happened."

"That must have been really upsetting."

"Well, it was even though, like I said, I didn't know the boy. But you didn't come here to talk about

Curtis Templeton, did you? What can I do for you?"

"No, you're right. I didn't come here to talk about Curtis Templeton. I just want to double-check some of the numbers that Ben wrote in the notes he left. We looked at his notes, and at Second Chance of Cobbs Creek's notes, and they're the same as far as attendance goes."

"That's right. They should be. Second Chance sends us their attendance data and that's what we use for our records."

"And – sorry if I'm covering ground you already went over with Ben – you use that data for school performance assessment?"

"No, that's the School District of Philadelphia's responsibility. In this office, we just manage the contract between the City and Second Chance."

"OK, I get it now. The programs you work with send you their attendance data and their other records, and you use that information to fund the schools and renew the contracts and that sort of thing, right?"

"Exactly."

"Does your office ever get involved with Second Chance's headquarters?"

"Well, the City's contract is with Second Chance, not with the individual centers. We do get some reports and things from the centers, but most of our communication is with headquarters."

"That's what I thought. And that's what I got from Ben's notes. So maybe you can help answer a question, since your office is in contact with headquarters. We found a difference between the attendance data we got from Second Chance of Cobbs Creek and the data we got from headquarters. But there was no difference between the Cobbs Creek data and the data we got from your office. Does that make sense?"

"I think the data is supposed to be the same. If it's not the same I'm not sure why. You'll probably have to ask over at Second Chance headquarters. Maybe they'll know."

"Maybe. Good idea. As you can guess, I'll be spending plenty of time there."

After a few more questions, Williams took his leave. He had a lot to think about and he wanted some peace and quiet. He took the elevator down to the ground floor of the Municipal Services Building and walked the two and a half blocks to where he'd parked his Dodge. He got in and sat for a few minutes as he absorbed what he'd learned. Then, he eased his car out of its parking spot and slowly made his way west through center city. Ten minutes later, he stopped at a coffee shop. After feeding the parking meter, he went inside and placed his order for coffee. He was sitting down with it when his phone hummed to life. He pulled it out of his pocket; the caller was Aaron Poole.

"This is Joel Williams."

"Joel, it's Aaron Poole, how are you?"

"Funny you called. I was actually just thinking of calling you. I think I may have something…"

Chapter Eleven

The next morning, Jered Carr stared blankly at *The Philadelphia Inquirer* spread out in front of him on the dining room table. Now and again he absently stirred his untasted tea. The night before, Lauren had told him about her fears and concerns about Mark Donnelly. She'd also told him about her conversation with that detective from Valley Forge. Even before Ben's death, Jered had wondered about Second Chance and some of the people associated with it. Now he was sure. What upset him most was that he should have seen it coming before Ben died. If he had, maybe he could have warned Ben. That thought had been haunting Jered since he and Lauren got back from Valley Forge and now he had no idea what to do with his sense of guilt. Lauren had told him that none of this was his fault and maybe she was right. Ben himself had suspected that something was very, very wrong with Second Chance, and hadn't been afraid to publish what the team had found. Nobody had known it all would end in Ben's death. But still, Jered couldn't shake a profound feeling that he should have done something.

He looked again at his newspaper. Maybe something there would take his mind off things. There was a story in the Local News section about a group of mothers who'd formed a home-schooling group and were taking turns teaching the children so that everyone could also work. Too bad Curtis Templeton's mother hadn't been able to home-school her kids. Maybe Curtis would still be alive. Damn! There he was thinking about the whole thing all over again. But wait a minute. Curtis' mother. Jered had gotten the feeling when he met her that she was holding back about her son's death. At the time, he'd thought she'd been paid not to press a negligence lawsuit against Second Chance or something like that. But what if it was more than that? Maybe she knew something. Why the hell he hadn't thought to go back and talk to her Jered didn't know, but then, he wasn't a cop. Well, no time like the present. He gulped his tea, not even noticing it was cold. Then he sent a text to Lauren. Pausing only to put on shoes and a windbreaker, he locked up the house and got into his Chevy. With luck he'd be at Shanita Finley's home within the hour.

"But I don't understand why you're talking to me at all about this," snapped Therese Vaughan. "I barely knew Ben Peterson – I spoke to him maybe twice or three times. And I never even met Curtis Templeton. How would I know anything about their deaths?"

"Well, it's just this, ma'am," Aaron Poole answered. "We're talking to everyone who's associated with Second Chance of Cobbs Creek and who was at the Riverton the other night. Just trying to get a sense of how it all fits together."

Poole had been glad when Joel Williams talked to him yesterday about Therese Vaughan. Here was a person who'd been at Second Chance of Cobbs Creek on the day Curtis Templeton died and at the Riverton when Ben Peterson died. It wasn't much, but Williams was right; it was something. Today was supposed to have been a day off for Poole, but ever since his wife Evie had died two years ago, days off hadn't meant that much to him. He found it easier to cope by keeping busy. So, he'd decided to take today and follow up on Williams' idea. He drove into Philadelphia late in the morning to avoid the worst of the drive-time traffic and went to the Municipal Services Building.

Now, he looked across the simple wooden office desk that separated him from Therese Vaughan. She looked right back at him, her temper regained but still smoldering.

"What makes you think those two accidents have anything to do with each other, anyway?" she was asking.

"That's exactly what we're trying to figure out – what connection there might be."

"Well, I honestly don't think there is one. Ben Peterson never met Curtis Templeton, did he? So, there's no way the two of them could have a connection. And anyway, it just doesn't make sense."

"Well, like I said, we're just trying to put the pieces all together. I appreciate that you took the time to talk to me about all of this."

Back in control now, Therese said, "Oh, not a problem. Was there anything else you wanted to know?"

"Not right now, no, thank you. I may be in touch, though."

"Sure. You know how to reach me."

"Thanks."

As soon as Poole had left her office, Therese Vaughan waited ten minutes to make sure he was safely gone. Then she pulled her telephone out of her purse and made a call. When she'd been connected, she said, "It's me...yeah, I know, but this is important...Look, there was a cop just here asking all kinds of questions.... No, but it's probably not going to be long before he pays you a visit....OK, well, I think we need to figure out what we're going to do..."

Once again, Jered Carr stood at Shanita Finley's front door. Once again, he was unsure of the reaction he'd get. He'd had time to think during the drive from Horsham. Yes, it was the right decision to talk to her again. She might have been paid not to talk to the press, but maybe she would talk to him. He knocked on the door and waited. Then he knocked again. After a few minutes, she opened the door. When she saw him, she said, "You back again? I thought we talked enough already."

"We did talk, but something else has come up. I'd really appreciate it if you could spare me just a few minutes."

"What's this about?"

"It really is important. Just five minutes, ten at the most. Please?"

She looked at him for a long moment, then held the door open for him. He thanked her as he passed into the living room. He hadn't noticed it the first time he was there, but now he was aware of the neat, well-kept room. The furniture was simple, and the green and tan sofa he sat on was worn and faded in places, but the pride the family took in this home was obvious.

"So, what's so important you need to talk to me about?" Shanita asked.

"There's been another death. A couple of nights ago, Second Chance had an Information Night for staff, investors, that kind of thing. My research team and I were invited to give a presentation. Right before we were supposed to present, one of my team members died. He – he went over a balcony and I think he was pushed."

"What's that got to do with me?"

"I don't know how to say this except just to say it. My research team and I were starting to wonder whether your son, Curtis – well, whether his death was an accident." Jered saw Shanita's face harden and hurried on. "No, please hear me out, OK? We got some background information on Second Chance for our study and the more we learned, the more we started to wonder about what happened to Curtis. We all started to ask ourselves whether Curtis' death was really an accident. Ben wanted to talk about Curtis' death at our presentation, and we were going to go along with that. He was killed before he could."

"So now wait. Are you saying you think someone killed Curtis? Pushed him on purpose? And that this man Ben Whatever was killed so he wouldn't talk about it?"

"I don't know that for a fact. I'm just saying that's what we're wondering."

"But who'd want to kill Curtis? And then somebody else, too?"

"Well, that's what I don't know. I was hoping maybe if I talked to you, you could help."

Shanita looked out of the living room window, then back at Jered. Then, after a bit, she said, "You really think somebody killed Curtis, don't you?"

"I don't know for sure. But yeah, I think maybe someone did."

She got up from the worn chocolate-brown club chair she'd been sitting in and went to the window. She looked out of it again for a moment, then said, "I'll be right back" as she left the room. Five minutes later she came back with two glasses of lemonade. "I should have thought of this before," she said. "Got a lot on my mind."

"Thank you," Jered said as he accepted the glass she handed him.

"I don't even know what to think," Shanita said after she'd taken a sip from her own glass.

"I know it's a lot to take in. I'm sorry I was the one to bring it up. I just -"

She held up a hand to interrupt him. "No, it's OK. Curtis was my son. If you're right about him, then I need to know."

"I'm glad you feel that way. I know this must be hard for you. Can you think of anyone at all who, well, would have wanted to hurt Curtis?"

"No. I mean, Curtis had a big mouth sometimes, and he got too bold. Did that to me, too. But he was a good boy. Nobody hated him."

"So, Curtis said things sometimes that he shouldn't have said. Do you think maybe he said something to the wrong person?"

"What do you mean?"

"I mean maybe he knew something, or saw something, and said something about it."

As he watched Shanita's reaction, Jered saw a look he recognized from his days as a parole officer. She wanted to tell him something but wasn't sure whether she should.

"If he saw anything, he didn't tell me about it," she finally said.

"Is there anything that he did tell you that might help us?"

[263]

Another long pause. "No, nothing he said."

"Then maybe something he did? Something that happened? Honestly," Jered put on his most appealing expression, "we could use all the help we can get."

"Look, if I could say something, I would. But I got my family to think about."

"Your family?" Jered said encouragingly.

"Yeah, I got other kids, you know. Me and my husband, we got bills to pay. Things we got to have."

"I understand exactly what you're saying. But anything you could tell us might help catch a murderer. And if your son was killed, it could help catch his killer, too."

"But you don't know he was killed, right?"

"We don't have positive proof. But that's what we think happened."

"But you don't know that for a fact?"

"Not yet. That's why I'm hoping you could help us."

"Look, I know you mean well, but I can't tell you nothing more about what happened to my Curtis."

A flash of inspiration. "Not even whether you got some sort of settlement?"

She looked steadily back at him. "Not about that, either."

Jered had met his match, at least for the moment. He didn't want to push Shanita Finley any further right now. Maybe he or Joel Williams or the police could talk to her again, maybe even convince her to help them. That wasn't going to happen, though, if she got her back up too much. So, he thanked her for the lemonade and prepared to leave. He'd gotten halfway to the door when she said one more thing. "If my boy was murdered, and you can really prove it, maybe you can come back then."

"If I can, I'll be back."

With that, he left the small rowhouse, smiling to himself as he made his way back to his car. Maybe he had gotten through, just a little.

Joel Williams pulled up next to Aaron Poole's unmarked National Park Service Jeep. Poole had called after his meeting with Therese Vaughan, and asked Williams to meet him at the 19th District

Police Station. Williams got out of his Dodge and, seeing that Poole wasn't in his Jeep, went across the street and into the police station building. Poole was inside the building's lobby waiting for him. The two men greeted each other, and Poole said, "I had them tell Carter Barclay that we're here. They said he'll be with us in a couple of minutes."

Williams nodded and thanked Poole, and then they both took seats to wait. About five minutes later, Barclay joined them. With him was another detective. She was of medium build, with coppery skin, dark brown eyes and straight black shoulder-length hair. Barclay said, "This is Julianne Yeadon. She was on the Curtis Templeton case and I thought she should be a part of this."

"Oh, absolutely," Williams said. He introduced himself and Poole and then said, "I really appreciate your letting us take a look at what you've got."

"Hey, if we can help each other…"

Barclay then led the way to a small, windowless room with institutional beige walls, equipped with a utilitarian wooden table and some folding chairs.

"Sorry I can't offer you a nicer place to work, but we're hurting for space and funding."

"This'll be just fine," Williams responded.

"You should see my cubicle," Poole said.

"Anybody want some of the mud they call coffee around here?" Barclay asked.

"Sounds good," Poole answered.

"Sure, thanks," said Williams. "It can't be worse than what they used to have at the Tilton police station."

"Yeah," Barclay said. "That stuff made dirt look appetizing. Julianne, how about if you tell Joel and Aaron what you know? I'll be right back."

Yeadon nodded. Barclay was trying to give her a chance to take the lead and she appreciated it.

"OK," she said as he left. "We got the report at two o'clock. The kid had fallen or gotten pushed off the scaffolding into the alley next to the building. It's a church now, I think. The lady who called in the report didn't see anybody or anything, but we asked around. We interviewed everybody, the whole thing. I'm not sure it was an accident, but we've never been able to prove anything."

Within a few minutes, Barclay had returned with coffee and the four were sitting at the table, shuffling through the piles of witness statements, forensics reports and summaries that told the story of the death of Curtis Templeton. For a long time, they read quietly, the silence punctuated only by the occasional riffle of a paper or scratch of a chair. Then Williams suddenly stopped and slowly re-read Therese Vaughan's statement, which he'd just finished.

"You know what?" he said when he was done. "Therese Vaughan was at Cobbs Creek on the day that Curtis Templeton died. She was also at the Riverton the other night."

"I remember," said Poole. "And she said she'd met Ben Peterson a few times. I see the connection there. But did she know Curtis Templeton?"

"She told us that she didn't know him," Yeadon said. "Said she found out about his death when she went over there for a meeting."

Barclay added, "And nobody could find a motive at the time, so it didn't go much further than that."

"I think there is a motive," Williams said.

Poole nodded, "If you and your team are right about Second Chance padding those attendance records, and she was in on it somehow…"

"Exactly," Williams said, looking appreciatively at Poole.

Barclay shook his head. "But that would mean that Curtis Templeton found out about the attendance and that Therese Vaughan knew he found out. If she works in the Municipal Services Building and he was over here at Cobbs Creek, how could she find out what he knew, if he knew anything?"

"I'll bet that wasn't the first time she'd been there. She could have known Curtis," Poole said.

"Maybe," Yeadon said.

"I can guess how Curtis found out about the attendance-padding, too," Williams went on. "He worked in the office at Cobbs Creek. That was his job. If he saw the records, he might notice the difference."

Barclay said, "You think a fifteen-year-old kid's going to pay attention to a few names?"

"He might if he saw the names of people he knew didn't go to school with him."

After a moment, Poole looked at the others, and said, "I think maybe I ought to talk to Therese Vaughan again."

Jered Carr thought about his conversation with Shanita Finley all the way home. If she had a settlement with Second Chance, that would explain why she hadn't said much about her son's death. But it didn't explain why Curtis Templeton had died. It was clear, at least to Carr, that Shanita Finley hadn't suspected her son was murdered. So, whatever the reason was for Curtis' death, she probably didn't know it unless she was a much better actress than Carr suspected she was.

When Carr got home, he settled down to reading some student papers that had been waiting for him. But after about half an hour, he found he couldn't really concentrate on what he was reading. His mind kept going back to Shanita Finley and what she'd said and didn't say. He finally tossed the remaining papers on the couch next to him and with a slight grunt, pulled his telephone out of his pocket and punched up Lauren's number. After he and Lauren had greeted each other, he said,

"You think you could find out something for me?"

"That would depend on what it is."

"I visited Shanita Finley again today –"

"– Curtis Templeton's mother, right?"

"Right. I could be wrong, but I don't think she suspected that Curtis was murdered."

"OK."

"But I think maybe she got some sort of settlement when he died, in exchange for her not suing, and keeping her mouth shut."

"Did she say that?"

"No, not in so many words."

"But you think she did."

"Yeah, I do. And if she did, whoever's behind the settlement could have something to do with Curtis Templeton's death."

"Don't you think that's kind of a leap?"

"Maybe. But after Ben's death I'm not so sure it is."

"OK, but where do I come in?"

"Can you find out anything about that settlement? Anything you could find out would help."

All of a sudden, Lauren's fears and concerns about Mark Donnelly came back to her in a rush. If there was a settlement, he'd know about it. He might even have the authority to approve it. Lauren felt her hands and feet grow cold and her stomach knot as she thought about what it would mean if Mark Donnelly was behind Curtis Templeton's death. And Ben's. She swallowed hard and from a distance, heard her husband's voice through the phone asking, "You still there?"

"Yeah, yeah, I'm here. Sorry."

"It's OK. So, will you see what you can find out?"

"Yeah, I will. Not promising anything, but I'll ask around a little."

"Thanks. See you at home. Love you."

"Love you, too."

Lauren slipped her phone back into her purse. The thought that Donnelly might be involved in Ben Peterson's death was bad enough. But that he might know something about Curtis Templeton's death – or even be involved in that – was more than she wanted to think about right now. Still, she'd told Jered she would see if she could find anything out.

She took a few deep breaths and stood up from the office chair where she'd been sitting when Jered called. After a minute, she felt ready. She left her office, closing the door behind her.

A few minutes later, Grace Wong looked up from her desk. She'd been Mark Donnelly's executive assistant for seven years and in that time, she'd become indispensable. A competent, unruffled professional, she seemed to rise above the stresses of a busy office and radiated calm competence. When she saw Lauren Carr at the door of her office, she said, "Oh, hi, Lauren. Come on in."

"Thanks. You got a minute?"

"Sure, what did you need?"

"I'm putting together a report for one of the school districts that might want to refer students to us, and I could use some information."

"OK." Grace turned directly towards Lauren.

"I'm hoping you'll know if there's some sort of resource we have for looking up information on Second Chance's history. Not just the "date founded" kind of thing that's in our brochures, but something with some detail."

"What kind of detail?"

"Well, this school district is a little concerned about security and safety. And lawsuits, I think." Lauren gave a short laugh. "So, they want information like number of lawsuits and settlements, any code violations, that kind of thing. Do we have a database that would have that sort of information?"

"Hmmm…" Grace's elegantly arched eyebrows puckered as she thought. "You could try our archived monthly updates. Those reports get compiled for Middle States accreditation, and they're pretty comprehensive."

"It sounds like a good place to start – thanks. How do I access the database?"

"Here," Grace said, reaching for a pen and a piece of paper. "Let me write it down. You know how to get to the employee resources web page, right?"

"Yeah, I do."

"Good. Here's what you do from there." Grace scribbled a few lines and handed the piece of paper to Lauren. "Let me know if you have any trouble."

"Thanks," Lauren smiled. "Appreciate it."

"No problem." Grace turned back to her computer and Lauren took the hint, smiling at Grace as she left.

Once she'd returned to her office, Lauren sat down at her computer and accessed the employee resources database. Then she followed Grace's instructions and within a couple of minutes, she'd found the archives Grace had described. She searched the archives for the time period she wanted, and soon found references to Curtis Templeton's death. She didn't find much that she didn't already know – just a paragraph or two about the incident and the steps Second Chance had taken in response to the death. There was mention of a meeting with Curtis Templeton's parents, but there were no details. Then she remembered that Mark Donnelly had been at that meeting.

That was it, then, Lauren thought. Donnelly would probably know about any settlement, if there was one. And Donnelly'd been at the Riverton on the night Ben died. If Ben found out about the settlement and was going to publish it as part of the paper, Donnelly could have… but wait a minute. That didn't explain what happened to Curtis Templeton. Lauren didn't think Mark Donnelly had ever met Curtis Templeton, let alone know him well enough to have a reason to kill him. And besides, although he sometimes did go out to the centers, Donnelly worked mostly out of his office at headquarters. But it was certainly possible for him to have been at Second Chance of Cobbs Creek on the day that Curtis Templeton died. And what about that theory that the research team had about padding the attendance records? What if Curtis Templeton had found out about that? Lauren couldn't see why the boy would say anything to Donnelly about it if he didn't know him, but you could never tell.

Lauren felt colder and colder inside as she thought about Mark Donnelly. All of the pieces were there and it all made her feel slightly nauseous. Still, just sitting and staring at the computer screen wasn't helping anything. Besides, she might be wrong. She finally took a breath, exited from the employee resources database and leaned over, picking up the purse that was lying next to her desk chair. She left her office, closing the door behind her, and went towards the elevator, hoping that nobody would see her. Luck was with her as she got into the elevator and headed for the ground floor.

When she got there, Lauren got out of the elevator and left the building, remembering too late that she'd left her blazer in her office. Well, she wasn't about to go back inside for it now. She walked a few feet away from the building, pulled her phone out of her purse and called Jered. When he answered, she said,

"Remember you asked me to find out about any settlements Second Chance has paid out?"

"Yeah, did you find something out?" Jered was alert now, hearing the anxiety in his wife's voice.

"I think I did. I checked our employee resource database. There wasn't much there, but it did say that some of the administrators had a meeting with Curtis Templeton's parents and even though they didn't say so, it seemed like there was a settlement."

"But it didn't specifically say so?"

"No, but listen, Jered, there's more. Those paragraphs reminded me of the day they came to headquarters. I'd forgotten about it, but Mark Donnelly was at that meeting. If there was a settlement – and it seems like there was – he probably knew about it…. Jered? Are you still there? Jered?"

"I'm here – sorry. I'm just trying to figure out what we should do next."

"I think we should tell Aaron Poole about this."

"Yeah, I think you're probably right."

"All right. Soon as I'm off the phone with you, I'll call him."

"OK."

Chapter Twelve

Aaron Poole pushed the "End Call" button on his
telephone and laid it down beside him on the front
seat of his Jeep. He'd just parked near the
Municipal Services Building where he'd planned to
tackle Therese Vaughan again when he got the call,
and it made him stop and think. Lauren Carr had
told him she'd found another possible link between
Curtis Templeton and Ben Peterson – Mark
Donnelly. He'd have been privy to any legal
agreement, and he'd met with Peterson more than
once. And nobody would have questioned his
presence at Second Chance of Cobbs Creek. If it
could be shown that he was there on the day Curtis
Templeton died, they might have something. Poole
tapped his fingers on the Jeep's steering wheel as he
thought about whether or not to go on with his plan
to see Therese Vaughan. In the end, he decided that
since he was in the city anyway, he might as well.
Still, he wasn't planning to ignore what Lauren Carr
had told him. He would go over to the Cobbs Creek
center tomorrow. That decision made, Poole got out

of his Jeep and locked it, then headed towards the Municipal Services Building.

When he got up to Therese Vaughan's office, Poole found that she wasn't there. Since the office door was open, he guessed that she'd probably be back soon and settled into a chair to wait. About ten minutes later she returned. When she saw him, she said, "Sorry, I didn't know you'd come back. I was just down picking up my mail and a copy job."

"Oh, that's OK. I only waited a couple of minutes."

"What can I do for you?"

"Well, it's about Curtis Templeton."

"Look, I don't want to be rude, but we talked about him already. I told you I didn't know him. I told you I didn't even know he was dead until I got over there that day. I'm not sure what else you want me to say."

"We're still trying to put all the pieces together, Ms. Vaughan. I'd really appreciate it if you'd go over your story just one more time."

"I've got to get to a meeting."

"I know you're busy. But I'm sure you want to help us find out who killed those two people, don't you?"

"Of course I do. It's not that. It's just that I don't know how I can help you. I don't know any more than I've already told you."

"How about you tell me again, just once more. It won't take long."

With an irritated sigh, Vaughan said, "All right. Like I told you, I never met Curtis. Didn't know him and didn't even know he was a student. I had a meeting at Cobbs Creek that day, so I went over there for that. When I got there, they told me that one of the students had had an accident."

"What did you do then?"

"I asked who it was, and they told me it was Curtis Templeton. I didn't know the boy, but I said something about being very sorry to hear it. I have a little girl of my own, so I felt for his parents. But that's all I know about that."

"And you left then?"

"I asked them to send me a copy of whatever report they'd send to headquarters about it, because I need that for my records. But I didn't stay long."

[281]

"And did you get that report?"

"About two weeks later, yes, I did."

"Could I see it?"

"OK, just give me a minute."

Poole waited while Vaughan walked over to her file cabinet, opened the third drawer and started flipping through its manila hanging folders. After a few minutes, she said, "Here it is," and handed a three-page document to Poole, who thanked her and glanced over the document briefly. He didn't read it thoroughly, but he could see that it didn't seem to contain anything he hadn't already learned about the day Curtis Templeton died. He asked, "Can I have a copy of this? Just for the record?"

"All right. Hold on a minute." Vaughan reached for the report and when Poole handed it back to her, she took it to the copy machine located in a small alcove in the hallway outside her office. After making the copy, she walked back to the office and gave the copy to Poole.

Then, Poole said, "The day that Curtis Templeton died, you said you had a meeting."

Vaughan nodded, "That's right."

"Who were you supposed to meet?"

"I'll be honest, it's been a couple of years, so I'm not sure I'm remembering right, but I think it was with Tim Dawson. Have you talked to him? He's the director over at Cobbs Creek."

Poole looked up from the notes he was making. "Thanks, I'll be sure and talk to him. OK, let's fast forward to Ben Peterson's death."

"I went to the Riverton, got there about six-thirty or so. I saw Mr. Peterson in the ballroom, but I didn't talk to him. The party got started and I saw him leave, but I already told you that."

"And you didn't see him again or speak to him?"

"No."

"Sure of that?"

"Look, Mr. Poole, am I a suspect? Because it's beginning to feel like you're interrogating me."

"Like I said, Ms. Vaughan, we're just trying to put all of the pieces together."

"Well, that's fine, but I didn't kill either Curtis Templeton or Ben Peterson. I didn't even really know them. Why would I want to kill either of them?"

[283]

"Maybe because they found out you were in on a plan to pad the attendance lists."

"Excuse me, but what are you talking about?"

"I think you know. Second Chance gets paid based on attendance. Second Chance of Cobbs Creek sends you a list with more names on it than there are students, so the company gets more money. You split that money with somebody at Second Chance in exchange for co-operating. That's how it was, isn't it?"

"I have no idea what you mean. I get the lists from Second Chance, and that's it. If those lists aren't accurate, it's not my fault."

"But if you participate in a scam like that, that's fraud and that's illegal."

"And I'm telling you I don't know anything about any scam."

Poole waited a moment, gathered his thoughts and went on. "Look, Ms. Vaughan, whether you want to admit it or not, you're in a lot of trouble. You were at the scene on the day that two people died. Both of those people can be connected to you. Your best bet now is to tell me everything. Everything."

"I didn't kill anybody. I had no reason to. Just because I went to the school on that one day, and was at the hotel, doesn't mean anything."

"By itself, no. But I'll bet there'll be a lot of official interest in those attendance records and in how Second Chance gets paid. Your personal financial records, too, I'd guess."

Therese Vaughan felt cold inside. Colder than she'd felt in a long time. She was going to have to say something, and she wasn't sure what. Aaron Poole wasn't going to give up; she could see that. "All right, look," she finally said. "You want to know who killed Curtis Templeton and Ben Peterson, right?"

"That's right."

"Well, I didn't. But maybe I can help you."

"That's what I'm hoping."

"OK, maybe I do remember a little more than I said before about the day Curtis Templeton died. But I'm a single parent. My daughter can't be without her mother. If I go to jail for fraud or whatever, that's what's going to happen."

"I can't promise you anything. I think you can figure that out. But I'm much more interested in finding out who killed Curtis Templeton and Ben Peterson than I am in tracing some money that got misdirected. That'll happen, but my main priority is catching a murderer. Help me with that and I'm pretty sure the District Attorney will take that into consideration."

"I want to talk to my lawyer first and see what she says. Then I'll have her call you. I hope that'll work."

Poole knew it was the best he was going to get for now. "OK, but the quicker this gets settled, the better."

"That's one thing we can agree on," Vaughan's professional mask slipped for just a moment and Poole could see the human person beneath it. Whatever else Therese Vaughan was, she was under suspicion of murder right now and it scared her.

After making sure she had his telephone number, Poole took his leave. He'd just have time to get out of center city before the beginning of afternoon rush hour.

Two hours later, Joel Williams pulled up at the Carrs' home. Lauren and Jered had invited him for drinks and dinner and he was glad not to have the drive back to Tilton that night. He'd have to leave early the next morning to back in time for the meeting with the dean, but at least he'd get a good rest.

He got out of the car, locked it, walked up the red-brick path to the door and rang the bell. Lauren let him in and within a few minutes, the three of them were seated in the living room with glasses of Beaujolais. It wasn't long before they began to talk about the one subject that was occupying all of their minds.

"I had a talk with Shanita Finley today," Jered began. "You know – Curtis Templeton's mother."

"What did she have to say?" Joel asked, his interest piqued.

"Honestly, it's what she didn't say. I told her about Ben's death and that it might be related to her son's death. Then I asked her if there was anything else she could add. She all but said there was some sort of settlement that came out of the whole thing, and that she couldn't talk about it."

"That makes sense if it was a settlement with a gag order."

"Exactly. But then I called Lauren, and – Lauren, tell Joel what you found out."

Joel turned his attention to Lauren as she gathered her thoughts.

"I didn't get specifics," she said, "because those are confidential. But about a week or a little more after Curtis died, his parents came up to headquarters. They had a meeting with a couple of our people at the top and Mark Donnelly was at that meeting. I remember that."

"So, if there was a settlement," Joel said, "Donnelly would probably know about it."

"Exactly," Lauren said. "And if he was a part of that settlement, he must have had a reason. It might have just been because he doesn't want Second Chance to get a bad reputation. But what if it was something more? What if he knows about the whole attendance thing? That's what upsets me. He's my boss. He's always been a real advocate for kids who need another chance, and I respected him for that. You don't think he could have killed Curtis and Ben, do you?"

"I know that he was there the night Ben died. And he could have been at Cobbs Creek the day Curtis Templeton died. But here's the thing," Joel continued, warming to the topic. "He's an administrator whose office is at headquarters. Does he ever go out to the centers?"

"Sometimes, but not really often," Lauren answered.

"OK, so if he were at one of the centers, it would be unusual, wouldn't it?"

"Well, it doesn't happen every day."

"Today I met with Aaron Poole and a friend of mine who's on the police force in the Cobbs Creek area. We were looking over the reports from Curtis Templeton's death to see if there was anything that tied in with Ben's death. None of the witnesses said that they saw Mark Donnelly at Cobbs Creek that day."

"Are you saying he wasn't there?"

"I'm saying nobody remembered him being there. And I have an idea that they would if he had been, just because it is a little unusual."

"God, I hope you're right!"

"Did you find out anything else?" Jered asked Joel. Joel, who was taking a sip from his wine glass, held up a finger and swallowed. Then he put his glass down on the coffee table and said, "I'm more certain than ever that the person who killed Ben also killed Curtis Templeton. I also think it's got something to do with the attendance padding we found. Curtis found out about it and somebody found out that Curtis knew."

"That makes sense to me, too," Jered said, "but why would he even notice attendance lists, much less pay any attention to them?"

"He might," Joel responded. "He worked in the office – that was his job at the school. He'd probably look for his own name first. That's just human nature. Then he might have looked for his friends' names. He could also have seen names he didn't know."

"It's possible, I guess," said Lauren.

"And if he did," Joel continued, "he might wonder why they were there." All of a sudden, he thought again about what that former student – what was her name again? Oh, yes, Marisol – what Marisol had told him. Curtis Templeton had been confused about something the day before he died. He'd said there was something he didn't understand. If he stumbled on those extra names, he might not understand them. And if he was curious at all, he might ask somebody in authority. Just then, Joel realized Jered had said something.

"Sorry, I was thinking about something. What did you say?" he asked.

"It's OK. I just asked if you wanted more wine."

"Oh, no thanks. Not just yet. To be honest, I was thinking about something that one of those former Second Chance students I interviewed said. She told me that on the day before he died, Curtis Templeton said there was something that didn't make sense to him."

"Did he say what it was?"

"No, that's the thing. She said he didn't. But I have the feeling it might have been something about the attendance padding. It just ties in with what she said."

"It sounds like it," Jered said.

The roast that the Carrs had planned for dinner was ready, so the three moved to the dining room and sat down. As they ate, they continued to talk about the murders.

"Did you get the feeling that Shanita Finley thought that Curtis was murdered?" Joel asked Jered.

"I really didn't get that idea at all, actually," Jered answered. "I'm not saying she was utterly shocked, but I don't think she'd thought about it that way before. I will say this, though. I'm pretty sure she is getting some sort of a settlement and she doesn't want to lose it. She didn't want to talk to me at all until I told her that there was a good chance that Curtis had been killed. And even then, she wasn't really willing to talk. She just said that if we found proof that Curtis was murdered, I could come back. I said I would."

"That's about what I would have expected," Lauren said. "She's trying to take care of her family. If she's depending on money from a settlement to pay the bills, of course she's going to keep her mouth shut."

"So even if she knows something about what happened, she's not likely to say anything," Joel mused.

"Not if saying something means she loses that settlement, assuming there is one," Lauren said.

"I'm not really sure she knows anything, anyway," Jered said. "I may be wrong, but I really don't think she suspected Curtis was murdered. If you're a parent and your child's been murdered, do you really keep your mouth shut?"

"That's the other thing," Joel agreed. "I don't think a lot of parents would just shut up and accept it if their child was murdered. But you never know. She might have her reasons for not saying anything even if she thought Curtis was murdered."

"Maybe," Jered said reluctantly, "But I just don't get the feeling that that's how it was."

The three finished their meal and Lauren and Jered began to clear the table. Lauren was carrying one of the serving dishes into the kitchen when she heard her tablet PC, which she'd left propped open on the table, announce an incoming video call from Mark

Donnelly. She put the dish on the counter, sat at the table and accepted the call.

"Hi, Mark."

"Hi, Lauren. Sorry to bother you at home. I hope I didn't interrupt your dinner or anything."

"No, that's fine, we were finished. What's up?"

"If you have a minute, I wanted to ask you about that information package you were putting together for the Christina School District."

"That's the Newark, Delaware district we're negotiating with, isn't it?"

"Yeah, that's the one. Their rep called about an hour ago and wants me to send her the package tonight if we can. She's got a meeting with the District Superintendent tomorrow morning and wants to read through everything first. Do you have everything ready?"

"It's all ready, but I'm not a hundred percent sure it's on my flash drive. Hold on a sec while I check, OK?"

"Sure."

Donnelly waited while Lauren checked the contents

of the flash drive attached to her tablet. Just then, Joel Williams walked into the kitchen.

"Anything I can do to help – Oh, sorry! Didn't know you were on a call."

"Yeah, sorry," Lauren said. "But this'll only take a minute or two more."

"OK."

Joel left the kitchen just as Lauren found what she needed.

"Mark? Thanks for waiting. I found the package. Do you need me to send it to the Christina rep or do you want it?"

"Could you send it to me? I'll make a copy of everything and then send it on."

"Sure, no problem."

"Thanks, Lauren, and sorry I bothered you at home."

"That's OK."

Mark Donnelly exited the video call and sat for a few moments staring at his computer screen. He'd clearly seen Joel Williams in the background at the Carrs' home during his conversation with Lauren, and that couldn't be good. In fact, that could be a

[295]

real problem. There'd likely be only one reason Williams was there: the research team was probably still asking questions. And it reminded Donnelly that Lauren Carr was married to one of the researchers. What if she was poking around, too? No, wait. He was being paranoid. There'd be no way she could be asking a lot of questions without him finding out about it. But still, it would be a good idea to take some precautions.

Donnelly spent the next half hour clearing out a number of files from his computer and uploading some others to his online storage account. Then, he went into his private email account and carefully sifted through that too, deleting several messages he thought it better not to keep. When he was satisfied, he made a phone call.

"It's me. Yeah, I know, but this is important. I think we need to watch what we're doing… No, it's that research team. They're still working on their study…exactly…Oh, he did? What did you tell him? …Good. All right, but…exactly. OK, we'll talk soon."

Donnelly finished his phone call and had just made another when he heard a tap on his office door and Grace Wong stuck her head in.

"You still here, Grace? I thought you had dinner plans."

"I do. I'm just leaving now. You need anything?"

"Nope. Thanks. Enjoy your evening."

"I will. You're not going to stay all night, are you?"

"No, I'm about to leave, myself."

"All right, then. See you tomorrow."

"See you."

Donnelly watched as his assistant quietly closed the door behind her. Had she heard his conversations? Probably not. Hopefully not. Who could ever tell? Would he have to tie up that loose end? That was something he hadn't thought about. How much did Grace Wong know? And had she told Lauren anything? He could at least find out whether she and Lauren had talked.

"Grace!" he called out.

She opened the door again, "Did you call me, Mark?"

"Yeah, sorry. I just thought of something. I'm supposed to send an information packet to the Christina School District in Delaware tonight. You know – the sort of package we send to all of the school districts when we're negotiating with them. Lauren Carr was working on getting everything together earlier today, but she didn't stop by my office with the finished packet. Did she give you a packet to give to me?"

"No, sorry, she didn't."

"Did she mention the information packet to you at all?"

"Well, she did say she was putting together a report for one of the school districts that came to Information Night. Maybe that's the report you mean."

"Could very well be."

"You want me to call her and see if she has it?"

"No, thanks. You go on. Don't be late for your dinner. I'll give her a call."

"OK, then, goodnight"

"Goodnight."

Donnelly felt a certain amount of relief at what Grace Wong had told him. If Lauren Carr was just working on that packet for the Christina School District, then she probably wasn't asking questions that were none of her business. But of course, you never knew. For the moment, Donnelly thought, things were all right, but that could change.

Donnelly was so lost in thought that he was startled by his computer's "Incoming Message" alert. He glanced at his screen and saw that it was a message from Lauren. Must be that packet he'd asked for. He opened the message and saw that he was right. He checked everything to be sure that the packet was complete. Then he checked it again, this time to see whether there was anything in there that was going to be a problem for him. There didn't seem to be. He prepared and sent the file on to the Christina School District representative. Maybe there was nothing to worry about after all. But still, Donnelly decided he was going to have to be very, very careful.

Chapter Thirteen

At nine o'clock the next morning, Joel Williams,
Shirley Mizzello, Charlie Nagle from the
Department of Psychology, and Fran Meisner from
Sociology, gathered outside Alicia Cardenas' office.
Cardenas rose from her desk and walked to the door
to meet them. "Come in," she said.

"Thanks for meeting with us," Mizzello said as they
went inside.

Once everyone was seated, the dean began. "So,
let's talk about this center."

"Well," said Nagle. "We have some real concerns
about the plans. We're hoping that we can discuss
them with you and get some answers."

Cardenas nodded and pulled a pad of paper and a
pen from her top desk drawer. "I'll just make some
notes while we talk," she said. When she was ready,
Nagle began.

"You mentioned in your announcement that our
faculty will be doing at least some of the research at
this new center. Is that right?"

"Absolutely. Faculty from the different departments will be doing collaborative and individual research."

"Then my question is this. How much input will YouthPromises have in our work? They'll have a stake, won't they, in our findings?"

Cardenas nodded again. She'd been ready for that question. "Academic freedom is a critical part of life at Tilton. YouthPromises knows that, and they've assured us that they will stay very 'hands-off' about the research."

Williams raised an eyebrow. "Do we have anything on paper?" Mizzello shot him a grateful look.

"Nothing's final yet," Cardenas said. "The paperwork isn't complete. But we can certainly consider adding in a clause about the independence of faculty research."

"I won't be comfortable supporting the center if there isn't some sort of protection," Mizzello said.

"OK," Cardenas said, looking up from her notes. "What other concerns do you have?"

"Mine's also a question about academic freedom, but from a different angle. How is this center going to impact what we teach?" Mizzello nodded vigorously at that.

"Well, there's certainly going to be a partnership between the center and the School of Social Sciences."

"But that's exactly what we're concerned about," Mizzello said. "Sorry, Fran – go ahead."

Meisner smiled a little. "Shirley's right," she said. "Members of the faculty determine the curriculum. That's part of our academic freedom, and it's in the Faculty By-Laws, isn't it?"

"It is," Cardenas said. "And let me assure you that no-one from the center will be writing your syllabi or designing your courses."

"Fair enough," Mizzello said. "But what about the content?"

Cardenas shifted a little in her seat. She glanced down at her notes and then said, "Well, we'd expect a close relationship between the center and the school, so we'd have a consistent approach."

Mizzello shook her head. "So that means there would be an impact on our content? An impact we didn't initiate? I would have a real problem with that." Williams nodded. He would, too.

"I have one more question," Nagle said as soon as Cardenas looked up again from her notes. "Who exactly will manage the center? Will it be Tilton people? YouthPromises people?"

"We're envisioning a center that's managed by a team composed of a few people from Tilton and some from YouthPromises. We'll also have some outside consultation from Penn State and the University of Maryland."

"So," Nagle said, "This isn't really a Tilton initiative, then?"

"Well, certainly we'll be heavily involved," Cardenas said.

"But this isn't a Tilton University project, managed and run by Tilton faculty and staff, right?" Nagle persisted.

"We don't want to be that insular," the dean responded sharply.

"Nobody's suggesting that we get no input from outside," Meisner said. "But if our research and courses are going to be impacted by this center, I think that raises questions of academic freedom." There were murmurs of agreement as the dean made some more notes.

[303]

"I appreciate your thoughts on this," Cardenas said, glancing at her watch. "I've made notes of what you had to say, and I'll bring it all up at our next meeting with the center's steering committee." Chairs scuffed softly across the carpet as everyone got up to leave. "When will we know a little more about all of this?" Meisner asked.

"I don't have an exact date yet," Cardenas answered. "But I will keep everyone informed." The group had to be satisfied with that.

Mizzello, Meisner, and Nagle left. This wasn't over as far as they were concerned. For a moment, Williams stood waiting to see whether Cardenas still wanted to talk to him. She did.

"Glad you could stay for a bit, Joel."

"Of course." As though he would have refused this sort of request from the dean.

"I wanted to talk to you in a little more depth about this center. You've got some background in the area of alternatives to juvenile prison, and I think that background would be a great fit with the center."

"I'm not sure I understand."

"Well, I'd like to put your name forward to join the center as a research consultant, but I wouldn't do it without your consent."

"What would that mean?"

"It would mean you'd be housed full-time at the center, and you'd do research on behalf of the center."

"What about teaching?"

"You'd be researching full time, so you wouldn't be teaching, unless you did a guest lecture or something like that."

Williams tapped a finger on the arm of his chair for a moment. He thought about the study he and Ben and Jared had been doing. Then he thought about Ben, and about Curtis Templeton. Finally, he said, "I'm not sure I'd be the best fit."

"In what way? I think you have exactly the background we need."

"I'm not sure whether for-profit alternative schools are the answer they were supposed to be, to tell you the truth. And I don't want to feel pressured to support them."

[305]

Cardenas thought for a moment. Then she said, "Look, Joel. I know you have some reservations about this. But it would be a real feather in your cap. And we need someone with your experience over at this center. YouthPromises wants the credibility. And we need them, too. It's a good opportunity for everyone. Besides, you could keep the center on an even keel – make sure the research is accurate."

Williams hadn't thought about it that way. Different points of view made research better, there was no doubt about that. "Besides," the dean added, "Some of these alternative programs do have positive outcomes."

"I know," Williams said. "In fact, my team and were getting some good preliminary results with the study we've been doing."

"There you go, then."

Williams shook his head a little. "I'm still not sure it's for me."

"Look, just think about it, all right? Don't say 'no,' yet."

"All right," he said after a moment. "You have made some good points. But I won't promise anything."

"That's all I ask."

Aaron Poole sat in his office going over the notes he'd made comparing the Ben Peterson case with the Curtis Templeton case. Joel Williams and his team were probably right that the two cases were connected. It had been good of Carter Barclay to let Poole use the 19th District's resources even though the Templeton case wasn't in Poole's jurisdiction. the more he found out about that earlier case, the more convinced he was that the same person had killed both victims.

Poole's review of his notes was interrupted by his ringing telephone. "Valley Forge National Park Service, Poole speaking."

"Ranger Poole? This is Lelah Drake from the Philadelphia District Attorney's office."

"What can I do for you?"

"I understand that you've been interviewing Therese Vaughan as a witness in a case you're investigating. Is that right?"

"That's right."

"I'm calling to let you know that our office and the Montgomery County District Attorney's office have reached an immunity agreement with Ms. Vaughan's attorney. Ms. Vaughan is now willing to assist your investigation."

Poole was busily making notes. "Can you send me a copy of the agreement?"

"We'll do that shortly. What's your email address, please? I'll send it that way, and then follow up with a letter."

Poole provided the information and thanked his caller. He wasn't overly surprised that there'd been an agreement, and he was fairly certain that Therese Vaughan knew more than she'd told him. But part of him was always a little bothered by immunity agreements. He didn't like it that this woman might be guilty of fraud and get away with it. Still, as he'd told her himself, he was interested in finding the person who killed Ben Peterson and Curtis

Templeton. If that meant Therese Vaughan wouldn't face prosecution for fraud, well, he'd have to put up with it.

Therese Vaughan slowly put her telephone down. Her lawyer had just told her that she wouldn't be prosecuted if she helped that detective with Ben Peterson and Curtis Templeton's murders. For a moment, she sat at her desk, staring at the picture of Nicole that was one of the few personal items in her office. She let the relief wash over her and thought about how very lucky she was. It wouldn't help her at all with paying Nicole's tuition, but there was nothing she could do about that right now. She'd have to find some other way to earn money. For now, she was going to have to meet with her lawyer and the detective and tell them. Just as well, as she thought about it. She hadn't wanted anybody killed. What she had done was one thing, but murder? Killing a person? That was totally different.

The meeting was scheduled for three o'clock in Valley Forge. That meant leaving the Municipal Services building by two or two-fifteen at the latest.

[309]

Therese reluctantly turned her mind back to clearing off her desk and finishing her to-do list, so she'd be ready in time.

By two forty-five that afternoon, Aaron Poole was ready for his meeting with Therese Vaughan and her attorney. They arrived on time and Poole didn't make them wait for him. As soon as they were seated in the wooden folding chairs in his office area, Poole began.

"Thanks for coming all this way to talk to me. I'm going to record this interview with your knowledge and permission."

Both women gave their consent and Poole turned on the recording equipment he'd prepared. Then he turned to Vaughan and asked her to give her name for the record, which she did.

"Ms. Vaughan, you're aware that you've been granted immunity from prosecution, so that you cannot be charged with any criminal act based on what you're about to tell me?"

"Yes, I am."

"OK. Did you kill Curtis Templeton or Ben Peterson?"

"No, I did not."

"Do you know anything about their deaths?"

"I didn't see them happen, no."

"But you know who's responsible?"

Vaughan turned to her attorney, who nodded for her to go on.

"OK, look. Here's how it happened. I was working with the Second Chance people to set up their contract with the City of Philadelphia. The way the contract is set up, Second Chance gets paid based on the attendance at each of the centers. The more attendance there is, the more Second Chance gets paid."

"Got it."

"A few of us saw that, well, we could make some money from the way that contract works. We, well, we put together a...financial arrangement. Second Chance of Cobbs Creek would send in certain attendance lists and I'd approve them. Then we'd split the extra money."

"You didn't have an arrangement like that with the other centers?"

"No, I only knew some of the people at headquarters and some of the people at Cobbs

Creek. I didn't want to depend on people I didn't know."

"Right, go on."

"Ben Peterson was on to the attendance thing. He put the pieces together and if he'd written it into that study, well, who knows what would have happened? I'm pretty sure he got pushed out of that window before he could say anything at Information Night."

"And what about Curtis Templeton?"

"He must have found out about it, too. He worked in the office at Cobbs Creek, so he must have seen one of the attendance sheets one day."

"OK, so who was in on this arrangement?"

Seventeen miles away, people were beginning to gather for a memorial service for Ben Peterson at the First Lutheran Church in Upper Darby. The Peterson family wasn't particularly religiously observant, but the church had a spacious social hall that could accommodate a large group. Besides, Peterson had grown up in Upper Darby and that was the church the family attended when they did go to services.

Right now, Ben's father Nate was getting comfort from the familiar surroundings, just as he had two years earlier when Ben's mother had died. There would be a private funeral the next day; this was to be a more public memorial service. Surprising, thought Nate, how many people were here already. Ben wasn't a hermit, but Nate hadn't realized how wide a social circle Ben had. This was going to be harder to get through than he'd thought. So many people, a lot of whom Nate didn't even know, would want to talk to him. Maybe he'd be ready for that at some point, but right now all he felt was hollow and empty inside. There just wasn't anything there. People didn't want to hear that, though. They wanted to connect. Wanted to feel like they were helping. Besides, it was a loss for them, too. The right thing to do was to be here and greet them. The emptiness would come back later, anyway. Nate straightened up, slowly got out of the pew he'd been sitting in, and moved towards the church doors.

Then the doors opened and in came his son Doug, who'd been given permission to attend the memorial service and funeral. Next to Doug was his prison escort. Nate hadn't seen Doug just lately, although he tried to visit him about once a month. Doug hadn't been able to stay out of trouble, and that hurt his father deeply. Nate had tried to set a good example and it just hadn't helped Doug. But still, he was Nate's son, and he'd just lost a brother and Nate wasn't about to make things any worse than they were. Now, he made his way towards his son and they greeted each other awkwardly.

"I'm glad you're here, Doug," Nate said. He was telling the truth, too. Whether he liked it or not, Doug was all he had left.

"Yeah, me, too. You OK?"

"Holding up."

"That's good."

"Can you stay long?"

"Sorry - they're taking me back right after the service, but I'll be back tomorrow for the funeral." Nate nodded in comprehension. "It's good you can do that."

Doug nodded and the two began to quietly greet some of the other people who'd arrived.

Joel Williams pulled open the church door and went in, grateful for the warm air that surged out as he did so. It was a cold, crisp day and there was a hard layer of frost on everything. Part of Williams didn't really want to be here. He wasn't one to put his grief on display for everyone and besides, the way he saw it, he'd played a role in Ben's death. He should have known that digging too deeply where you weren't welcome could be dangerous. He should have warned Ben to be careful. He hadn't. What could he possibly say to Ben's father? He was not looking forward to the obligatory greeting.

Just as he was trying to figure out how he was going to bring himself to speak to Nate Peterson, Williams felt his phone buzz in his pocket. He pulled it out and saw that the caller was Aaron Poole. Forgetting the frosty weather outside, Williams turned around and went back out of the church.

"This is Joel Williams."

"It's Aaron Poole. I hope I caught you before the service starts."

"You did. The service doesn't start for another twenty minutes."

[315]

"Good. Listen, I just got finished interviewing Therese Vaughan."

Now Williams was even more attentive, pacing up and down the walkway leading to the church as he talked. "What did she have to say?"

"Turns out you guys were right about the attendance padding. She told us all about it and how it worked. She and Sheldon Adler and Mark Donnelly were in it together. They split the extra money that the company got from the City of Philadelphia for those extra names. And she told us that Ben Peterson had found out about what they were doing."

"And I'll bet Curtis Templeton did, too."

"Yeah, and she had more to say. On the night Ben Peterson died, she and Sheldon Adler were standing in the lobby of the Riverton talking when they saw Peterson come across the lobby. He was heading towards the ballroom when they saw him and talked to him for a few minutes. They tried to talk him out of mentioning Curtis Templeton's death, but he was adamant. Then she said she saw Peterson head towards the elevator. She was going to go up after him to do some damage control. Adler told her no, he'd talk to Peterson when he came back

[316]

downstairs. The two of them went back into the ballroom together, but here's the thing. She says Adler said something about making a call and left the ballroom."

"So, he wasn't in the ballroom when Ben died."

"That's right."

"And he works at Cobbs Creek."

"Yes, he does."

Now Williams realized he'd been wrong about who was responsible for Ben's death. And probably Curtis Templeton's death, too. He struggled to hear the rest of what Poole was saying as he mentally cursed himself. Finally, he gave up and said, "I'm sorry. Could you say that again?"

"I was getting ready to ask you to do something. You OK?"

"Yeah, just feeling really idiotic. I missed some things and my thinking just plain went the wrong way on this."

"We've all done that."

"I know. Doesn't help much, though. But what did you want to ask me about?"

Poole returned to the topic. "I'm guessing several of the Second Chance people are going to be at that memorial service, right?"

"Probably. Staying away would be pretty bad for their PR."

"That's what I think, too. If Adler's there, and he probably will be, keep an eye on him, will you? You've been a cop, you know what I mean. See if he says anything or does anything we should know about. I'd really like to get some direct evidence on this guy before I go any further. I'm coming down myself, but I probably won't be able to be there until the service is over."

"Oh, believe me, it'll be my pleasure."

Mark Donnelly and the top administrators at Second Chance had asked several of the staff members to be at Ben Peterson's memorial service. It wouldn't look good, they said, if Second Chance didn't have a presence there. Some people, like Lauren Carr, had gone in to the office to keep things running. But several Second Chance people where there. Sheldon Adler hadn't wanted to attend the service; funerals and memorial services always made him uncomfortable. But he hadn't been given much choice. Besides, Donnelly and other people from Second Chance were there, and his absence would have been noticed. So as the service began, he joined the rest of the people filing into the pews.

The service wasn't very long, less than an hour. Still, Adler had begun to feel restless by the time the minister had finished speaking. Then Peterson's father went up to the front to speak. That must have been hard for him, and he didn't have much to say. You could see he was numb – almost somewhere else. Then some of Peterson's other relatives came up and said a few things. Adler couldn't much keep his mind on what everyone was saying but he was surprised at how many people there were. Peterson hadn't struck him as the outgoing type. He watched the chilly late afternoon sun slant through the windows on each side of the church and got through the service as best he could without calling any attention to himself.

When the service finally ended, Adler moved with everyone else down a staircase from the church's

[319]

sanctuary to the social hall one floor below. Some volunteers from the church had prepared coffee and tea and set up tables of food, and after a few uncomfortable moments, people began to make their way to the coffee and hot water urns. Within a short while, the strained near-silence had given way to the muted sound of low-toned conversation. In ones and twos, everyone made a point of speaking to Nate Peterson, who was sitting at a table with the minister.

Adler was working out in his mind whether he could avoid speaking to Nate Peterson and if he couldn't, what he'd say. Just then, he felt the beginnings of a sneeze. Fortunately, someone had thoughtfully placed a few boxes of tissues in the room and Adler grabbed a few from the nearest box. When he'd finished sneezing, he prepared to put the ones he hadn't used into the pocket of his suit jacket. Something else that felt like a piece of paper was already in the pocket and he pulled it out to see what it was. When he opened it, his face went pale. That was when he remembered he'd worn the same suit the night Ben Peterson died. He hastily folded the paper up and thrust it back into his pocket. He glanced quickly around him and, when he saw that nobody was watching him, he left the room. He needed the restroom.

Joel Williams had been paying close attention to Sheldon Adler during the entire memorial service. He'd managed to find ways to stay nearby without calling attention to himself, so he was only a few feet away when Adler sneezed. Williams saw him pull a piece of paper out of his pocket and open it. When Williams saw Adler's reaction, he stepped a little closer and saw what it was – a copy of the handout Ben had planned to give out at the Information Night presentation.

After what seemed like a century, but was really less than three minutes, Sheldon Adler found the restroom. He yanked on the handle to open the door, but it wouldn't budge. It was only then that he noticed the sign on the door saying "Push." He pushed on the door, it opened, and he rushed in. He glanced around for an empty stall, found one and headed for it. He pulled the handout out of his pocket, crumpled it up and aimed for the toilet. Before he could release the balled-up paper, though, his wrist was grabbed from behind and a voice, low but fierce, said, "No, you don't! That's evidence." Adler whirled around and looked into the hard face of Joel Williams.

"What the hell are you doing?" Adler snapped angrily as Williams grabbed the paper.

"I said that's evidence. You can't destroy it."

"Evidence of what? What are you talking about?"

"Evidence in the murder of Ben Peterson."

"You must be crazy! It's just a piece of paper – it's nothing!"

"Let's let the police decide that."

"The police? Now I *know* you're crazy. Look, this is a memorial service for someone you knew. Don't you think that's affecting your judgment?"

Williams said again, "Let's let the police decide that."

Adler waited a minute or two, and when Williams didn't say anything more, he said sullenly, "You know, you can't keep me here."

Williams looked steadily at Adler but said nothing. He'd learned the value of silence when it came to getting people to say things they wouldn't otherwise have said. Besides, he could tell that Adler was getting unnerved. He didn't have to say anything.

Adler looked around. There was only one door to the restroom and there were no windows. If he was going to get out, he'd have to pass Williams, and it wasn't likely that Williams would just let that happen. He couldn't stay there, though. He started to move forward, but Williams moved, too, blocking his way.

"It's not worth it," Williams said quietly but firmly. For a moment Adler stood there. Then he suddenly shoved Williams in the chest and rushed past him out of the restroom.

Aaron Poole left his Valley Forge office just after he'd finished talking to Joel Williams and had made a few other phone calls. A frosty twilight had begun to settle, but the road was clear, and he was lucky to be driving in the opposite direction to the surge of traffic leaving Philadelphia. Within forty minutes he'd reached Upper Darby and had soon found the church. Hoping he wouldn't be too late, he hastily parked and got out. He rushed towards the church just as the front door flew open and Sheldon Adler ran out. Adler started towards his car, but Poole soon blocked his way.

"Mr. Adler, I'd like to talk to you about the death of Ben Peterson."

"I had nothing to do with that, and anyway, I've already told you everything I know."

"I still have a few questions, if you'll come with me, please."

"You can't arrest me! I didn't do anything!"

"Mr. Adler, you're not under arrest at this time but we do need to talk. I need for you to come with me, please."

By this time, several other people, among them Joel Williams, had begun to leave the church. In twos and threes, they made their way to their cars. When Williams saw Poole and Adler, he smiled grimly to himself and walked over to where the two men were facing each other.

"You might find this useful," he said to Poole, and handed him a folded paper towel. Poole nodded and lifted the edge of the towel to see what was inside. It was a crumpled-up piece of paper. Poole looked questioningly at Williams.

"It's a copy of the handout that Ben was going to use for our presentation on Information Night," Williams explained. "He never got a chance to pass them out, though. He didn't have them with him when we met before the dinner, so my guess is, he left them in his room. I think that's why he went back to his room right before he died – he wanted to get the handouts."

Poole quickly picked up on Williams' thinking. "If you're right," he said, not taking his eyes from Adler, "then there were only two people who'd be likely to have that handout: Peterson and his killer. How did you get that handout, Mr. Adler?"

"Ben gave it to me."

"But you said you didn't see him once the dinner began. He didn't have the handouts then, so how could he give one to you?"

"I – I –"

"Mr. Adler, we need to talk about this. A lot. I'm going to need you to come with me."

Adler finally nodded and walked to Poole's police car. The fight seemed to have gone out of him as he got in.

It took an hour to get back to Valley Forge because of the traffic. During the whole trip, Sheldon Adler was silent, and Poole was glad for that. He was tired to begin with, and he wasn't really interested in whatever excuses or explanations Adler might make. He wanted this case to end.

It was completely dark and getting cold when Poole and Adler arrived at the small building where Adler's office was located. Still silent, the two of them got out of the car and went inside. Poole nodded a greeting to the receptionist and the two men went back to Poole's cubicle. When they got there, Adler was shocked to see Therese Vaughan and another woman already sitting near Poole's desk.

"What are you doing here?" Adler asked, suddenly feeling as cold inside as it was getting outside.

"Ms. Vaughan and her attorney are here about the Ben Peterson case, just like you are," Poole said. "Now that we're all here, how about you sit down, Mr. Adler, and we'll get started."

"I don't know how I can help you," Adler said as he slowly sat down. "I've already told you everything I know."

"Oh, come off it, Sheldon," Vaughan said wearily. "Don't waste your time. I already told them about everything."

"What are you talking about?"

"Stop it!" Vaughan insisted. "It's over, OK? It's over."

Poole said, "Ms. Vaughan told us about the financial arrangement you had with her."

"Financial arrangement?"

"Yes, about the attendance data."

Adler could see that Poole wasn't bluffing. One look at Therese Vaughan's face was enough to show him that she'd told Poole everything, and he gulped as it hit him. That bitch! She hadn't been able to keep her mouth shut. Adler was going to have to think fast. After a moment he said, "OK, so maybe I had a little arrangement with a few people. It didn't really hurt anyone, and it doesn't mean I killed anyone."

"But it gives you motive," Poole pointed out. "Ben Peterson found out about the attendance padding. You found out he knew."

"She had as much motive as I did," Adler fired back, glaring at Vaughan. "And she talked to Peterson just before he died."

"So did you!" This came from Vaughan, who added "I was right there with you, too, so don't try to deny it. And then you left the ballroom. I saw you leave. You had the time to kill Mr. Peterson before I saw you again."

"Why are you doing this to me?" Adler asked.

"You're setting me up! She's setting me up!" he said to Poole.

"No, I'm not," Vaughan said firmly. She lifted her head and went on, including both her lawyer and Poole in her glance as she spoke. "Look, I did something I'm not proud of. I took money. I had my reasons, but I did it. But I never planned for anyone to get hurt. I never meant for anyone to get killed. That's something I wouldn't do."

Adler said, "Well *I* didn't kill anybody!"

"Yes, I think you did," Poole said. "Ms. Vaughan
here saw you leave the ballroom. You had a
handout that you wouldn't likely have had unless
you'd been up to Mr. Peterson's hotel room. Here's
what I think happened. You went up to Mr.
Peterson's room. You had an argument and pushed
him out the window. Maybe you hadn't planned it
but that's what happened. You noticed you still had
a handout and stuffed it in your pocket. You forgot
about it until today at the memorial service."

"You're wrong – all wrong," Adler said, but his
voice was less assured than it had been.

"I don't think I am."

Adler looked around at the faces staring back at
him: Poole's calm and impassive, Vaughan's hard
and inflexible, her attorney's alert and attentive. He
watched as Poole placed the paper towel holding the
handout on the desk in front of him. Then Poole got
up, went over and stood directly in front of Adler.

"You want to tell me what really happened, Mr.
Adler?"

[329]

Vaughan's attorney quietly said, "I think we're done here. We'll be in touch."

Poole nodded without looking away from Adler as the two women rose to leave.

Adler watched them go and then dropped his head onto his hands.

Chapter Fourteen

When Joel Williams got the call later that night, he was sitting in the Carrs' living room. They had invited him to stay with them instead of in a hotel and he was grateful. It spared him the long drive back to Tilton, and he had plans in the city the next day. He'd just finished telling them about the memorial service when his telephone buzzed. He pulled it out of his pocket and saw that Aaron Poole was calling.

"Hey, Aaron, how did it go?" Williams asked, getting straight to the point.

Not one to waste words, Poole responded, "We got what we needed. We got him for Peterson's death."

"That's good," Williams answered.

"Yeah, he told us what happened. According to Adler, he never intended to kill anybody, but when he went up to Mr. Peterson's hotel room, they got into an argument. He tried to convince Peterson to leave the whole Curtis Templeton thing and the attendance thing alone. Even admitted he tried to buy him off. Didn't work, and they got into it. Next thing he knew he'd pushed Peterson off the

[331]

balcony. Said he didn't notice that the window was open until it was too late."

"You believe him? That it was accidental?"

"It could've happened that way."

"Yeah, it could have. Thanks for telling me."

"I figured you ought to know. The one thing that gets me, though, is that we've got the guy for Peterson's death, but we don't have anything to tie him to the Curtis Templeton case. I need real evidence to go after him for that."

"I'll bet if you work with Carter Barclay and the people over at the 19th, you'll get what you need."

"Yeah, you're probably right. It gets me, though. You know what I mean?"

"Yeah, I do."

The two finished their conversation and then Williams told the Carrs what he'd learned. Jered looked away for a moment and muttered, "Bastard."

"I'm just glad they got him," Lauren said. "And I have to admit, I'm glad it wasn't Mark. I just didn't want it to be a guy I've worked with, and who I thought really wanted to help kids."

"Mark's still going to have a hell of a lot to answer for," Jered said.

"I know. It's probably going to cost him some jail time and his career," Lauren answered. "But it's not the same as killing somebody."

"No," Williams said. "It's not."

Then, Williams shifted a little in his seat, and said, "Do you really think Mark Donnelly wanted to help students? That that was his main goal?"

"I always thought so," Lauren answered. "Why?"

"I'm beginning to wonder about these for-profit alternatives, that's all. After everything that's happened, I'm just not sure what I think."

Jered nodded. "I know what you mean, Joel. Our study found some promising things, but –"

"That's just it!" Williams interrupted. "They do have promise. Maybe it was just these people, at this time."

"Maybe."

After a moment or two of quiet, Lauren asked, "Why the question about Mark?"

"I'm trying to figure out what I think of these for-profit alternatives." Williams leaned forward and continued. "I've been offered a chance to be a part of a new center that Tilton's hosting – a center for research on these kinds of alternatives to juvenile prison."

"That sounds like a real opportunity," Jared said.

"It is," Williams nodded. "But the thing is, it's going to be funded by YouthPromises. Have you heard of them?"

"Just barely."

"They run a whole string of alternative schools and programs, and they want a center at Tilton to give them some research backing. I just don't know if I can be the one to give it. Not after all of this. But Second Chance did seem to get good results. And it's not the only program that does."

"Maybe it's not the concept itself. It's more about the people," Lauren said.

"Now, there might be an interesting research angle," Jered said. "The people who make these places work well."

Williams lifted his head up a little. "Could be interesting. And maybe working at the center would give me – us – the chance to look into that a little more."

At six-thirty the next morning, Joel Williams left
the Carrs' home and drove into Philadelphia. He
would have liked to go to Ben's funeral, but at least
Jared and Lauren would be there. For once, he
drove without the radio on. He wasn't at all sure
what he would say to Alicia Cardenas. It might be a
good thing to work at the center, do some research,
and get a better picture of these for-profit programs.
Some of them could really help young people.
Besides, it might be nice to take a break from his
usual routine. But then there were the students he
wouldn't teach. The very real issues his colleagues
had with the center. And his own doubts.

Williams got to Cobbs Creek within an hour, still
not sure what he would do about working at the
center. He stopped thinking about that problem,
though, as he got closer to the building where Curtis
Templeton had died.

What had been a construction site was now home to
the Cobbs Creek Church of the Gospel. When
Williams got to the church, he walked past the front

of it. He didn't really expect to see anything of interest there, but he did notice that the side of the building faced an alley. That must have been the side where the boy had been pushed. The other side was too close to the next-door building.

Williams went around the corner and walked past the part of the building that faced the alley. He looked up at the third floor. That's where Curtis Templeton had to have been when he was pushed off. And nobody had seen anything. Williams glanced up and down the alley. Across from the church was Atlas Payday Loans, a check-cashing and payday loan company. Williams was sure he remembered reading that when the police had originally investigated Curtis Templeton's death, they'd talked to the people on duty at Atlas that day. They hadn't seen anything, but that wasn't surprising since the front entrance to the store didn't face the alley. He walked back to the front of the building and up the three steps to the church door. He thought it would be locked but to his surprise, it opened when he pushed it.

He went into the church and looked around. It wasn't decorated elaborately, but it was clean and well-cared-for. The stained-glass windows let in shafts of pale morning sunshine, but most of the church's sanctuary was dim. Williams was just deciding how much to look around when a voice behind him said, "Can I help you?"

Williams turned around. The voice belonged to a short, slight woman with close-cropped, curly black hair and deep brown eyes. She looked steadily at Williams as she waited for his response.

"I hope I'm not intruding," he responded. "My name's Joel Williams. I'm a professor at Tilton University, a couple of hours west of here."

"I'm Lydia Enfield. I'm the assistant pastor here. What can I do for you?"

"I've been working on a study of Second Chance – the alternative school. Have you heard of it?"

"Yes, I know it."

"Then you may know that a couple of years ago, a kid from Second Chance –"

"– fell off some scaffolding from this building. Yes, we all know that story."

[337]

Williams smiled a little. "I thought you probably would. The boy – his name was Curtis Templeton – was a student at Second Chance of Cobbs Creek. My research team and I found out about his death while we were getting information for our study."

"And how can I help you?"

"Well, it's just this. We found out that Curtis Templeton didn't fall. He was pushed."

"You mean someone killed him?"

"That's what I mean."

"Oh, that's terrible! It's bad enough he died so young, but to be killed? That's horrible!"

"There's something else. It looks like whoever killed Curtis Templeton has killed someone else. A friend of mine named Ben Peterson. He was one of the members of our research group."

"I'm so sorry. That must be hard." Lydia Enfield's expression softened a bit.

"It is, thanks. The police found the person who killed him, and now they're looking for evidence that'll connect that case to Curtis Templeton's death."

"And you think you'll find it here?"

"I don't know. The building was under construction at the time, and I can see you've made a lot of changes to it. But I thought a quick look around wouldn't hurt."

The assistant pastor seemed to come to a decision. "All right," she said. "You can go ahead and look around. I'll come with you."

"Thank you." Williams didn't blame her for wanting to go with him.

Together, the two walked around the sanctuary. Williams' guide pointed out a few things of interest there. Williams admired the hand-varnished oak benches and stained-glass windows. Then they went up to the second floor of the building, where the church offices and a few Sunday School classrooms were located. It was easy to see that much more money had been spent on the sanctuary than on the offices and classrooms. They were clean and well-organized, but utilitarian and spare. Williams glanced out a few of the windows as he had the opportunity, but he didn't see what he'd been hoping he would see. When they'd finished the tour of the second floor, Williams asked, "Is there anything up on the third floor?"

Enfield hesitated, then said, "We usually don't take people up to the third floor. Is there some particular reason you need to go up there?"

"I don't want to make anything uncomfortable for you. It's not even the rooms themselves I'm interested in. I'd really just like to look out the windows."

"The windows? Why?"

Now it was Williams' turn to hesitate a moment. "I want to see whether anyone could have seen what happened to Curtis Templeton."

Enfield thought for a while. Then she said, "OK, I'll show you."

Williams followed her up a staircase at the end of the second-floor hall. The third floor of the building looked more like a storage area than anything else. Enfield explained, "Our Board of Directors has been thinking about turning this floor into a temporary shelter for abused women and their children. We haven't gotten the official approval, so we don't have any funds right now. I'm hoping that

[340]

will change. For now, though, we're using the floor to store extra chairs and things until we get the go-ahead."

"I hope you get the approval."

"Me, too. I've been trying to convince the Board to do this for a while. But you're not here to listen to me talk about our plans. You said you wanted to look out a window?"

"If you don't mind. Do you happen to know which window…?"

"Yeah, I think it's this one." She guided him over to one of the windows and he glanced out.

For a few moments, Williams just looked out the window. It faced the alley, so he could see clearly the building on the other side. He stuck his head out the window and looked left and right, too, to get a sense of what was there. Then, he pulled his head back in and asked Enfield, "Do you know anything about that cash place across the alley?"

"Not much. I know they've been there for, oh, five, six years, something like that. Longer than we have."

"Do you know if they have the whole building?"

"That I don't know."

"That's fine. I can always ask them."

"You think that may have something to do with that boy's death?"

"Maybe. I'm going to find out."

Williams thanked Enfield and the two of them went back down to the church sanctuary. He left the church and hurried across the alley to Atlas Payday Loans. A sign on the door announced that the store wouldn't open for another hour, so Williams crossed the street and had a muddy cup of coffee at a dismal café. While he waited, he glanced at the headlines on a copy of the paper that someone had left behind.

When the loan company opened, Williams went back across the street and went to the counter. From behind a Plexiglas window, a young woman looked up and said, "Can I help you?"

"I hope so. Can I talk to your manager, please?"

"She's in the back. I'll get her."

The young woman disappeared into a back room. Three minutes later another woman, this one middle-aged, with mid-length straight brown hair and wearing a dark pantsuit, came out of the back office.

"I'm Suzanne Hargraves. I'm the branch manager. Is there something I can do for you?"

"I'm Joel Williams. I'm a professor at Tilton University, a couple of hours west of here."

Williams took a business card out of his wallet and slid it through the small opening in the window. "I've been working on a study in this area and I have an odd sort of question for you."

The branch manager's eyebrows went up as she waited for Williams to continue.

"It's about a death that happened across the alley a couple of years ago. I don't know if you ever heard of it or not, but a boy named Curtis Templeton fell off some scaffolding when the church over there was under construction."

"Oh, yeah, I remember. The cops came in and talked to us."

"I figured they would have. I just have one or two other questions I'd like to ask if you don't mind.

Part of my report includes what happened to that boy, and I'd like the facts straight."

"I'm sorry, but I don't think I can help you. I mean, we were open when it happened, but nobody saw anything. The entrance doesn't face the church."

"Does your business use the third floor of this building?"

"The third floor? What's that got to do with anything?"

"Curtis Templeton fell from the third floor, and one of the windows on your building's third floor faces the church's third floor window."

"It does? Yeah, I guess it does. I don't think about it much because we only use that room as a counting room. The only time anyone's in there is when a shift ends, and someone has to count out. Otherwise the room's locked. Nobody would've seen anything unless they were counting out when the kid died. And besides, whoever's in there is counting, not looking out the window."

"That makes sense." Williams thought for a minute and then said, "If your counting rooms are anything like the counting rooms in banks, they have video cameras, right?"

"That's right. We need that for security."

"Exactly. Are those cameras on all the time?"

"Twenty-four hours a day. And they're motion-sensitive, so whenever there's movement, they focus on whatever's causing it. Why? Oh! You think maybe one of our cameras might have caught something?"

"It's a possibility. If one of the cameras faces the window. Is there one that does?"

"Yeah, one faces in that direction, towards the window, and the other is on the opposite wall. It faces the door. Hey, you sound like a cop."

"I used to be one. Guess it sort of stays with you. Do you keep archives of what that camera that faces the window picks up?"

"Our Asset Protection people do. The security camera feed is stored in digital files, and the AP people look at them if they need to."

Williams nodded. "I think I get it. Thanks."

"You think I should tell the cops about those cameras?"

"I have a friend who's a cop. I can tell him, and he'll probably want to come and take a look at your archives."

"All right."

Williams left the payday loan company and walked back to his car. He pulled his phone out of his pocket and called Carter Barclay, who was just coming back to his desk from morning report.

"19th District, Barclay."

"Hi, Carter, it's Joel Williams."

"Oh, hey, Joel. What's up?"

"I think I have an idea of how we can find out what really happened to Curtis Templeton."

"What do you mean?"

Williams told him.

Two hours later, Williams returned to Atlas Payday Loans. This time, he'd brought Carter Barclay and Julianne Yeadon along. Williams and the two detectives went into the store and asked to see Suzanne Hargraves. She was with a customer when they got there, but joined them within five minutes. After Williams introduced his two companions, Hargraves looked from one to the other for a moment and then said, "You're here to see those video files, right?"

"That's right," Yeadon answered. "I wish I'd thought of asking to see them two years ago."

"Me, too," Hargraves answered. "Nobody thought of it. Not videos of the counting room."

"Well, we're here now," Williams said.

"Right," Hargraves answered. "Let's go."

Hargraves led the four of them up to the second floor of the building, where the server and some offices were. They stopped in front of one of the locked doors. Hargraves took a set of keys from her pocket and opened the door to a small office that held a few computers. She chose one and turned it on.

When the computer finished booting up, Hargraves accessed the program she needed to look at the video files they needed.

"These are the files from Camera A in the counting room," she explained. "That's the one that faces the window. What date do you need?"

Yeadon answered without having to think about it. It was burned into her memory. After a moment or two, Hargraves had found that date's archives.

"Do you have a time?" she asked.

[347]

"We don't have an exact time," Yeadon said. "The coroner's report put the death at between ten o'clock that morning and one-thirty that afternoon."

"Good enough," Hargraves said.

She isolated the files from the third-floor counting room for those hours and one by one, accessed them. As each file came up, everyone watched to see if anything would show up. The first hour's file showed nothing. The camera hadn't picked up any activity. The second and third hours' files weren't any more helpful. Everyone was beginning to wonder whether this was a wasted visit when Hargraves began to play back the videos from the hours between noon and one-thirty. Then, while they were watching the second-to-last video – the one taken between twelve-thirty and one o'clock – Barclay noticed something. "Check that out," he said, pointing at a figure slowly appearing on the scaffolding across the street from Atlas.

"It's pretty far away," Yeadon said. "Can you zoom in?"

"Just a minute," Hargraves said. Within a moment or two she'd zoomed on the image of Curtis

Templeton. Yeadon didn't have to wonder who it was; she had his picture burned in her memory, too. "That's him," she said softly.

Barclay gave her an encouraging look, then turned back to Hargraves. "Keep going. Maybe we'll see something."

Hargraves nodded and resumed the video. Within a minute or two, the boy was clearly visible on the scaffolding. Then, slowly, another figure came into view. The figure moved closer to Templeton.

"We got him!" Barclay said.

"Yeah," Yeadon looked back at him. "We do."

Williams and Hargraves watched with the police officers as the video showed Sheldon Adler push Curtis Templeton off the scaffolding.

Yeadon swore. "This was here the whole time," she said, "And nobody thought to ask about it!"

Williams said, "Don't do that. It wasn't an obvious thing. It happens that way sometimes."

"I know, but we should have thought of this."

"You can't think of everything," Barclay said. "And the big thing is we got him now."

"Yeah, that's true," Yeadon said. "Doesn't help much, though. But," and she looked up at

Hargraves, "I'm really glad we got the guy. Thanks for telling us about this video."

"If I'd thought about it at the time, I'd have –"

"I know, you didn't think of it. We didn't think of it. But we'll use it now," Yeadon said. "I'm afraid we're going to have to take this hard drive and the camera. You'll get both back, but right now, they're evidence."

Hargraves said, "Look, I want to be helpful. I really do. A boy got killed and my camera got the killer. But I need to talk to my Asset Protection people and have somebody come out here. They're in Center City, so it shouldn't take too long. Do you want to come back?"

"I'm afraid we can't do that, ma'am," Barclay said. "But we don't mind waiting."

"All right. Let me make a call."

Early that evening, Sheldon Adler sat with his lawyer in a small conference room at the jail where he was being held. They were preparing for his arraignment, which would start in a short while. Adler's lawyer said, "The D.A.'s office is going for a murder charge, but I think we can get them to go for manslaughter. You didn't go up to that hotel room planning to kill anybody."

"No, I didn't," Adler said distractedly.

"Look, I know this is hard for you, but you have to stay with me. We might just get a real break here."

"Sorry. This is just…too much for me. I can't believe this is really happening. I mean – look at me! I'm in jail!"

"I know, it's stressful. But I'm doing my best for you, and I think we have a chance to get those charges reduced. You'll have to focus, though."

"I know, I know. I'll try."

"Good. OK, now, let's talk about what's going to happen now…"

The two had only been talking for about five minutes when the door of the conference room opened, and Julianne Yeadon walked in. Both men looked up. She was going to enjoy this.

"Sheldon Adler?" she asked.

"Yes, that's me," Adler answered.

"I have a warrant here for your arrest on the charge of murdering Curtis Templeton." Then she began to recite Adler's rights.

[351]

"Wait just a minute," his lawyer said when she'd finished. "What the hell are you talking about? Sheldon, what is she talking about? You need to tell me everything. Now."

"But I didn't! I have no idea what she means!"

"Mr. Adler," Yeadon went on, "we have a video of you pushing Curtis Templeton off some scaffolding at the Cobbs Creek Church of the Gospel."

"But that's impossible! There wasn't a –"

"Shut up!" Adler's lawyer hissed at him. "Don't say anything else!" Then he turned to Yeadon. "What exactly is this video you claim to have?"

"It's more than a claim," Yeadon answered. "There's a payday loan place across the alley from where the scaffolding was. It's got security cameras on all the time, including the day that Curtis Templeton died. Your client was seen on camera, pushing the victim off the scaffolding."

The next few minutes were a blur to Sheldon Adler. He heard his lawyer talking with that police officer but couldn't make sense of what they were saying. All he could think about was that someone had a video. A video! But there hadn't been anybody around. It had been perfect. After that stupid kid had asked him about those extra names on the attendance list, he'd told him he'd take care of it. He'd even thanked him for mentioning the names and told him to take the afternoon off – he'd cover for him. And he had. How could there be a damned video after all this time!? By the time his thoughts came back to what he was hearing, the cop had finished talking and looked as though she were ready to leave. As she turned to go, she said, "I'll see you at your arraignment, Mr. Adler."

When she'd gone, Adler asked his lawyer, "So, what do we do now?"

"Now? With two deaths, and one caught on video? I'll be doing a good job if I get you thirty to life."

Adler slumped down in his chair as his lawyer began going over what would happen next.

Chapter Fifteen

Joel Williams and Jered Carr stood with Julianne Yeadon and Carter Barclay in the lobby of the 19th District's headquarters. Carr said, "I really appreciate your letting both of us come along with you."

"It's OK," Yeadon answered. "You two were a big part of this. You should be there. I'm going to have to give the official notification, though."

"Of course," Williams said.

The three took their leave of Barclay, with Williams promising to call him soon. Then Williams and Carr got into Carr's Chevy, and Yeadon got into a black-and-white cruiser.

Shanita Finley heard the doorbell ring for the second time. She peered out of the window of her bedroom, where she'd been getting ready for work, but from that angle she couldn't see who the visitor was. She saw a black Chevy on the street outside, but it wasn't familiar. Then she saw the black-and-white cruiser pull up behind it. When the doorbell rang for the third time, she went downstairs. She looked through the eyehole in the door and saw that researcher who'd asked her questions about Curtis. Jered Carr, yeah, that was his name. And there was someone else with him, too, some other guy. And a cop. She recognized her as the cop who'd asked her questions when Curtis died. She slowly opened the door and looked from one to the other.

Yeadon spoke first. "Ms. Finley, I think you remember me. And you've met Mr. Carr, right? And this is Joel Williams, who's been working on the Second Chance research project with Mr. Carr. May we come in for just a minute? I've got some news that I think you'll want to hear."

"And what news is that?"

"Could we please come in? I think it'd be better that way."

A little reluctantly, she nodded and opened the door, stepping back to let her visitors inside. She led the way to the small living room and said, "I don't want to be rude, but I got to go to work soon. I hope this won't take too long."

"It won't," Yeadon answered. The three sat down and Yeadon went on.

[355]

"Yesterday the police arrested a man for murdering Curtis. They got clear evidence that he's responsible."

"Who...who was it?"

Williams and Carr looked at each other, but it was Yeadon who answered. "It was Sheldon Adler."

"Mr. Adler? He killed my Curtis? Why?" Despite her best efforts, tears started to form in Shanita's eyes.

Williams answered this time. "Curtis had found out about some illegal financial things that were going on at Second Chance. Mr. Adler was involved in a fraud scheme and Curtis found out about it."

"And Mr. Adler killed my boy to shut him up? Is that what you're saying?"

"That's right. And I am so sorry for your loss," Williams answered.

Shanita stared into space for a moment, trying to control herself. Then she said, "You know, when Curtis got into trouble, we thought Second Chance was such a good thing for him. He wasn't a bad boy, just needed some discipline. We thought that school would help him straighten up. When he died, the people at the school came to his funeral. They made a settlement, too. I needed that, because I got other kids. And now you're telling me somebody at that place killed him…"

Nobody said anything. There wasn't really much to say. Finally, she continued. "I should have been there. I thought he was safe."

Then Williams spoke. "Please try not to blame yourself. You couldn't know."

"Maybe not, but it seems like I should have."

"I sort of understand," Williams said. "We think the same man killed our friend Ben Peterson, the other person working on this research project. Every day I wish I'd said something or done something differently."

Carr looked out the window for a moment; Ben had been his friend, too.

"Look, I got a lot to deal with. And I got to get to work. I don't want to be rude, but…"

"It's OK. We should get going anyway," Carr said.

Shanita Finley walked with Yeadon, Williams and Carr to the door and then looked for a long moment at Yeadon. She saw the pain in Yeadon's eyes and realized for the first time that Curtis' death had hurt this woman, too. "Thank you for telling me what happened to my boy. It's good to know the truth." Yeadon nodded. The two men said their goodbyes and then the three of them left.

Therese Vaughan signed off her online bank account. It was going to be hard to manage for the next couple of years. For one thing, she would have to find a new job. As soon as the news had gotten out about what she'd done, she'd been fired. But at least she and her attorney had worked out a deal with the D.A.'s office so that she could pay back the money and the fines a little at a time once she did get work. And she wouldn't be going to jail. That was the best thing, of course. Then there was Nicole's father, too. The court had finally tracked him down to some little town across the river in New Jersey. He and his lawyer had fought against paying extra for Nicole's school tuition. They'd said she didn't need that program. But Therese had the paperwork now to prove she benefited from it. They had a court date set for next month. It wouldn't look good that she'd been caught in that attendance thing with Second Chance, but her lawyer could help her with that. She'd see what happened once the judge made a ruling in the child support hearing.

That evening, Jered and Lauren Carr sat at their dining room table finishing a bottle of Syrah. Neither had said much over dinner, but now Lauren spoke.

"I want to talk to you about something I've been thinking of for a while now."

Jered looked up.

"I think I want to leave Second Chance. I've been looking at ads, and there are positions out there for people like me who have experience in for-profit education companies. But I'm not even sure I want to stay in that business. Not after what's happened."

"I don't blame you. The whole thing's been horrible."

"It has, Jered. First, Curtis getting killed – murdered! And then Ben. And then we find out it was all because of an attendance scam, and my own boss was involved! Mark Donnelly has taken an 'indefinite leave of absence' from Second Chance. He said he had 'personal reasons,' but I know it's about this whole attendance thing. Some people from the D.A.'s office came in to audit everything this morning."

"Are they going to interview you?"

"Probably. I don't know yet for sure. I know they talked to Grace Wong for a couple of hours."

"You think she was involved?"

"I'm not a hundred percent sure, but I don't think so. I think – I hope – it was just Mark in our office. But see? That's why I want to leave. I don't know. I just don't know."

"What do you think you'll do?"

"Well, I'm thinking of going for career counseling. I want to take stock of myself and see what I'd like to do."

"That makes sense. And if you need any classes, Delaware River offers free tuition for faculty family members."

Lauren smiled at her husband. "I just might take you up on that."

Doug Peterson flipped through the pages of Caesar Rodney College's catalogue. He'd never made any plans before – not any real, lifelong plans. As he looked at the course selection, he thought about all the time he'd wasted. He was already close to thirty and hadn't even gotten an official high school diploma. He'd been in prison long enough to know he didn't want to make a career out of living there. He was going to have to do something. He wasn't sure exactly what yet, but he knew how he was going to start. He found the Criminal Justice Department's section and leafed carefully through it until he found his brother's picture. Slowly and carefully, he tore the picture from the catalogue and put it on the small table in his cell. Twenty minutes later, it was time to go to his weekly meeting with one of the prison's counselors. When he got there and sat down, his counselor asked, "So what would you like to talk about this time?"

"I want to take some classes. I want to get my high school diploma. Then we'll see."

Aaron Poole got a courtesy call from Julianne Yeadon. She told him that Sheldon Adler had been arrested for Curtis Templeton's murder, and how they'd found the evidence. He thanked her and the two agreed to exchange copies of their files on Adler. They'd be co-operating on mounting

[361]

prosecutions against him for both Curtis' and Ben Peterson's murder and both of them knew it was best to work together.

Shanita Finley got off the trolley and pulled up the hood of her jacket. It was getting cold and she was going to be outside. She walked the rest of the way to Old Cathedral Cemetery where Curtis was buried. She went there a few times a month to put flowers there and make sure his grave was clean. She couldn't stay long today; it was awfully windy and anyway, she wanted to get back home. Tonight, she was going to a special dinner and she had to get ready. Temple University and one of the local banks had teamed up to set up a college scholarship fund in Curtis' memory for Cobbs Creek students, and they'd invited her to the announcement dinner. It wasn't her kind of event, but for Curtis' sake, she'd go. Now, she wound her way along the cemetery paths until she found her son's grave. As she got close, she noticed a young girl, looked to be about Curtis' age, walking on one of the nearby paths. She wasn't very near, but Shanita could see her lift her

[362]

hand to brush it across her eyes. Poor kid. Whoever she'd lost, Shanita hoped she would find peace.

That was odd. There were already some flowers on Curtis' grave. The supermarket kind, but they were pretty. That was nice, that someone else remembered her son. Shanita wondered who it was, and for minute, thought again of the girl she'd just seen. She was gone now, but it was good to know that Curtis' friends were thinking about him.

Shanita laid the chrysanthemums she'd been holding on the grave and then sat down next to it, even though the ground was cold. In her own way, she told Curtis about the scholarship fund. She told him about the visit she'd had from that police officer and those researchers too, and what they'd told her. When she'd finished, she straightened up with an effort and got ready to leave. Curtis was still gone, but she at least had let him know she found out what happened to him. That gave her some peace. The rest would have to wait.

Joel Williams exited from the Pennsylvania Turnpike onto the local roads that would take him back to Tilton. He was looking forward to getting back. He missed his wife, he missed his dog, and he missed being at Tilton. Still, tomorrow morning's department meeting with Ed Beaumont would be difficult. Whichever decision he made about working with the center, there'd be people upset with him. He wasn't looking forward to that.

He hurt, too. He'd almost forgotten how much police work could hurt you. That was something they didn't teach in a lot of criminal justice programs. On top of that, he still thought of Ben. A lot. He was going to have to cope with that, and it wouldn't be easy.

Ben. Of course. Ben was a born researcher. He'd have wanted to ask the questions and find out the answers. He'd have wanted the center. With a slight nod of his head, Williams made his choice. As the scenery changed to the hills and farmland of Eastern Pennsylvania, he started to relax just a little. After about forty-five minutes, he pulled over for a rest stop. When he was finished, he picked up his telephone.

"Alicia? Joel Williams…Fine, thanks, and you?… Good…Yes, I'm on my way back to Tilton right now. I should be there in an hour, and back on campus tomorrow morning for an early meeting…That's exactly why I'm calling. Do you have a minute? …Great, thanks. I have one question about the center. How much control would faculty researchers have over what they study and how they go about it?"

About the Author

Margot Kinberg is a mystery novelist with many years of experience in higher education. Don't miss her other Joel Williams novels, *Publish or Perish*, *B-Very Flat*, and *Past Tense*! Connect with Margot at her official web site or on Facebook or Twitter.

www.ingramcontent.com/pod-product-compliance
Lightning Source LLC
Chambersburg PA
CBHW072113250626
47159CB00007B/2435